Jamie's Keepsake

M Gallagher

Copyright © Michael Gallagher 2020, who asserts the moral
and legal rights to be identified as the author of the Work.
This edition printed independently.
ISBN: 9781712435724

All rights reserved. No part of this publication may be
reproduced, stored in an electronic retrieval system, or
transmitted in any form or by any means without the prior
written permission of the publisher, and may not be otherwise
circulated in any form of binding or cover other than that which
it is published and without a similar condition, including this
condition, being imposed on any subsequent publisher.

This novel is a work of fiction. Any resemblance to actual
persons, dead or alive (except obvious public figures) is purely
coincidental.

Every effort has been made to ensure that there are no
outstanding rights issue. If any are identified, these shall be
corrected in a new edition.

Cover photo provided by maximimages (c) alexmaxim
Cover design layout by Jordan McGinlay.

Names have been changed to protect the guilty.

Author's Note

After a forensic analysis and report on the *Lady in a Fur Wrap*, (BBC News November 2019), the famous portrait is no longer being attributed to the artist El Greco. It is the work of another 16th century master, Alonso Sánchez Coello, apparently.

Hardridge

Alex Hannah emptied the bag of going home clothes onto the hospital bed, got dressed and stood blushing at the sight of himself in his dead brother's things.

'Ma kept thinking you were gonni die an all,' Forbes said from the visitor's chair.

He spoke again when Alex didn't answer. 'Will it be sore?'

'Eh?'

'Getting dead.'

'What?'

'Will dying be the sorest thing ever?'

Alex took a moment. 'If a hoose fell on you,' he said. 'That'd be sore. Or if a steamroller ran over you... aye, you'd be dead forever if that happened. Dead flat.'

Giggling, Forbes put his hand over his mouth, but couldn't stop himself. He clenched his eyes, drew in a deep breath and let out a cackling, shouldn't-be-laughing laugh. 'Dead flat!' he said and laughed harder. It set Alex off too.

By the look on the sister's face, she was ready to scream at them as she returned from the office with Da. Everyone in the ward was staring, and Forbes was still at it, his sleeve in his mouth to muffle his giggles.

Da got in first, 'Cut it out you two.'

Being taken round the beds to say cheerio to each of the boys added to Alex's unease. They were just like him. Leaving was all they ever talked about, how they'd be running around the streets with their mates getting into all sorts of bother. Now, like him, they weren't saying much.

'He's a bit down because he'll miss you all,' the sister announced. 'Not to worry, for he can come back and visit anytime.'

Alex thought about that as he walked from the Southern General with Forbes and Da to the bus stop at Govan Cross. He wasn't sad, and there was no way he was going back to visit. Whatever was niggling him was getting better with every step he took.

The number 49 dropped them off at the housing scheme, Hardridge, a bright and clean place — the summer sunshine and clear blue sky helping that first impression.

The new flat was four lampposts up the hill, past neat hedged gardens and rows of maroon-painted balconies on tenement walls speckled with brown and yellow pebbles, and up three flights to the top landing.

'You alright?' Da asked.

'I'm good,' Alex said, puffed out after climbing the stairs.

Ma was in bed. She pushed herself upright, held out her arms and snatched him into a tight hug. 'I've prayed to Jesus every waking minute.'

Her cuddle delighted him, although it went on a bit. 'You can let go now, Ma.'

She ran her palm over his cropped head. 'You're like a new pin. I hardly recognised you there.'

'The comb kept tugging, so the nurse goes and gets the clippers and scalps me.'

'It's a pure baldy,' Forbes said.

Next to the bed, baby Sarah lay in the cot. She stared wide-eyed and pedalled her podgy wee legs as Alex lifted her and dangled her above his head and made faces at her. 'She's got chubby jaws and slanty eyes like you, Forbes.'

'Shut your yap. You mean she stinks like you.'

Da took the baby, held her at his shoulder and spoke to her. 'You're a wee smasher, sure you are?'

When Alex asked if he could go outside, Ma gave a worried look. She hugged him again, and he didn't protest.

'He's to get plenty of fresh air,' Da said. 'It's doctor's orders.'

'Only if you promise to stay within shouting distance.'

'Aye, Mammy. I will.'

'And don't mention TB. Say it was tonsillitis if anyone asks.'

He checked out the flat. It had a kitchen with a porthole looking onto the balcony, a bathroom, a living room and three bedrooms, one empty apart from a sewing machine. Nothing much to see from the bedroom windows, just the back gardens of the tenement blocks and the criss-crossing lines of washing hanging in the sun. The view from the front was more like they'd promised — over the roofs of terrace houses to open countryside and a pine forest high on a hill.

Forbes came to his side. 'Guess who's flitted here?'

'Dunno.'

'See if you can guess.'

Alex shrugged a shoulder.

'Jamie.'

'Bryce?'

'Aye. He says he's going back to raid the empty hooses. Says you've got to be a good climber to do all the roof jumps and that.'

Ripping lead pipe and flashing from the roofs of the derelict tenements and selling it for scrap was a scary way of making money when they lived in the Gorbals. Jamie had even gone on night raids with the older boys, across the rooftops of the warehouses in Plantation and Tradeston. Alex liked hearing their tales — sneaking around at night, steering clear of the polis and flogging their knocked off stuff to neighbours, saying it fell off a lorry.

'We can do the roof jumps as well as anybody, sure we can?'

'Aye,' Forbes replied. 'I think we can.'

Alex noticed a dog sitting on the steps of the terrace houses. He loved dogs. He went with Forbes to pet it but took second thoughts once he got down onto the street. It showed its teeth and growled at him, a massive brute of a dog with ugly knotted veins on its face and legs and battle scars on its mangy yellow fur.

A blonde girl came from the house and sat next to it.

'Alright Forbes?' she said, while squinting at Alex. She seemed about fourteen, his age.

'Alright Coggie?' Forbes replied. 'He's my big brother.'

Alex kept his distance.

'What's the matter? Feart it's gonni come and bite you?' she said.

'Nah, I'm feart it's gonni come and eat me.'

'He won't hurt you unless you try anything. Walk up slow and let him sniff your arm.'

Alex stayed put. 'Is he yours?'

'He doesnae belong to naebody.'

'What's he called?'

'Homeless.'

'Homeless?'

'Aye, Homeless. Someone took him into the scheme in a van and chucked him out and left him to fend for himself.'

'Where does he sleep?'

'Anywhere.'

'What kind is he?'

'My daddy says part Bull Mastiff... but since I've never met one of them, I wouldnae know. He follows me around.'

The dog stood when she did, watching her.

'D'you want to go see George Best?' she said.

Alex screwed up his face.

'The fitba player,' she explained.

'I know who he is.'

'He's in my hoose.'

'Get away.'

'You get.'

'The Man United player?'

'See for yourself. My big brother painted him. He's at art school.'

'Oh, right,' Alex said, still not sure what she was on about.

She wagged her finger at the dog and told it to stay, then led the way upstairs. 'He isnae allowed inside.'

The name on the door said Coghlin. She used a key and yelled, 'Nathan!'

Nathan stuck his head into the hall. He was older than his sister, maybe seventeen, blonde hair like hers, only his was long and held back in a hippy headband.

'They're here to see George Best.'

'Cool,' Nathan said and went back inside, leaving the bedroom door open.

Going to see a student's artwork was the last thing Alex would've wanted to do after just getting out of hospital, but he changed his mind as soon as he walked into that room. The late afternoon sun flashed up colours on every wall, colours on paintings that dazzled and lifted his mood for some reason.

The football painting was different from the others — George Best's shirt the only colour on the canvas, shimmering like red-hot coals and standing out against the grey shadows of the roaring crowd as he turned from goal, arm raised.

Alex touched the canvas. The paint was lumpy, not smooth like it seemed.

'Nathan's getting a tenner for that,' Coggie said.

Forbes let out a low whistle. 'A tenner! That's more than my old man's dole money.'

'Is George Best worth more than the Beatles?' Alex asked.

'Depends what you like. He's oil. The Beatles are watercolour. By the way, he was wearing a blue jersey when he scored that goal in the European Cup Final a few years back. I changed it to scarlet, the proper colour for Manchester United.'

'I'd never sell him,' Alex said.

Nathan took a packet of cigarette papers from the pocket of his denim shirt, reached under the bedside cabinet for a tobacco tin and sat back, cross-legged. 'I can always do another,' he said as if it was easy.

A painting of Coggie was propped on top of the cabinet. The image made her blue eyes stand out against her blonde hair and freckles. When Alex turned to check the likeness, she tilted her head and posed a smile like in the painting.

There was more to see — shelves stacked with jars of coloured powders, brushes, paints, crayons, chalks and scrapers, a motorbike poster stuck on the ceiling and a 'Ban the Bomb' sign on the door.

'How come paintings cost so much?' Forbes asked.

Nathan smoothed out a cigarette paper. He placed tobacco on top and rolled it between his fingers. 'Some are worth nowt and some thousands. The most famous in the world would cost you a million.'

Forbes put his hands in his pockets and pulled them inside out. 'Sorry, don't have that much on me, ha ha.'

'It's called the *Mona Lisa*. It got nicked from this museum in Paris. Guarded by security men with guns, and this Italian guy walks right in and unhooks it and waltzes right out with it under his arm. He took it home on the bus. Cool, eh?'

'Did he get caught?'

'It was like a royal princess had been kidnapped... a big fuss, all over the papers, rewards, everybody hunting for it. He surrendered in the end.'

'Who's he?' Alex said, pointing to a drawing of a man in a green combat jacket and black beret with a red star in the centre.

'That's the freedom fighter, Che Guevara. Fought for the poor against the capitalists until the government assassins done him in.'

'Don't listen to him. His head's full of the commie mince he gets from my daddy.'

'Shut your yap, Shona. You're a parrot, copying Mammy.'

'Do they teach you to paint like that at art school?' Alex asked.

'They don't teach me nowt. They're all posers in that place. They hardly even talk to you. They're into all this modern art crap. It's kid-on stuff. I won't be doing it. I'm—'

He dropped the unlit roll-up and covered it with the bed sheet as the door opened.

A woman walked in. She'd been listening. 'You better watch your step, Nathan Coghlin, or they'll kick you out on your ear and you'll have to pay back your bursary. Then where will you be? Tell me that.'

She looked at the two boys. 'No one from these streets ever gets the opportunity he's getting. And this big lazy lump thinks he's too good for it! Thinks he knows it all.'

'Go away, Mammy,' Nathan said.

Missus Coghlin held the door. 'Show your friends out, Shona. I want a quiet word with your brother.'

Coggie walked them to the foot of the stairs. 'Don't bother about her. She's always moaning.'

Alex wasn't sure how to reply. 'All mammies are moany, sure they are?' he said.

'Mine's the moaniest.'

Forbes tugged on Alex's arm after she turned back upstairs. 'That isnae true. Ma hardly says nothing about nothing. She kept thinking you were gonni die an all.'

'Stop saying that!'

'Da says she'll get better now you're back.'

They sat on the couch that evening, eating from plates on their knees, mince and tatties and carrots that Da had cooked. Alex couldn't finish his. He dumped it in the bin and went to the bedroom and cuddled up to his mother. She put her arm around him. He had missed her more than anything.

As he lay there, his mind wandered, thinking of the torment when she didn't come to see him for months. He would have done a runner then, if not for the dopey jabs that made him float in and out of the dopey dreams. He remembered waking up, pulling the tube from his nose and staggering around the ward jabbering and pointing, the night terrors. The psychiatrist visited him at that time, holding his hand and asking loads of stupid questions, nodding and smiling and lying — he wasn't to feel let down by anyone, he'd soon be back with his family, home before he knew it, in a new house well away from the smelly slums. It was a lie because they kept him for the best part of a year, in the same hospital, same ward, where his brother had died.

Rope Swing

Alex woke with a parent on either side. It felt like the safest place in the world. Nothing could hurt him. Then it felt embarrassing — only babies sneaked into their parents' bed. He rose and went to the kitchen and pulled a chair to the window, knelt on it, wiped away the wet from the glass and cradled his chin in his palms to watch the morning.

The edge of the sky was pink, yellow and pale blue from the sun that hadn't yet risen above the trees, the road silent. Silent until the milk float came whirring down the hill and braked, causing the bottles to clap in the crates. A round of applause to awaken the street. The big dog raised its head from the shadows and barked.

Shying well clear of it, the milk boys darted up the stairs with two and three bottles in each hand. Alex watched until they turned the corner. Not long after, men began leaving for work, all going in the same direction, down the hill, queuing at the bus stop and getting hurled away in the green and orange corporation buses.

When Sarah began whimpering in her cot, Da got up and came into to the kitchen in his pyjama bottoms. 'Dressed already. You off somewhere?' he said.

'Waiting for Forbes.'

'Could be a while. Best to give him a shout.'

After making up the baby's bottle, Da ran it under the cold tap, tasted it to make sure it was cool and took it to the bedroom. He came back after a while and got the frying pan going. The spatter and smell of it must have lured Forbes, who hobbled in, half asleep.

'This isnae the Ritz. You don't get breakfast in bed in this hoose.'

Forbes rolled his eyes. 'He says that every morning.'

It was gone eleven by the time the boys left the house. Their father saw them out, warning them about the river and the railway, and making them promise to stick together. Their mother was still dosing.

Small white moths floated up at their feet as they waded through the knee-high grass to the foot of the hill below the pine forest.

Forbes scampered ahead. 'Race you up!'

Alex took it slowly, the sun on his face and beads of sweat on his forehead. It was heading for a scorcher. He rested halfway then on the ridge at the top.

Behind him, Forbes dropped from a tree. 'C'mon, I'll show you the river.'

On the far side of the forest they reached a cow field overlooking the river. It glinted in the sun, not much of it because of the bushes and trees on the bank, but enough to trace its shape past playing fields and curving out towards the hills. In the opposite direction, it disappeared under a jungle of trees that spread for miles.

'That's the park,' Forbes said.

'You could get lost in there.'

'You could... do you know when you're out and you've forgot your compass?'

'Oh aye, that happens all the time.'

'Well, you can find your way if you check moss on a boulder. It tells you which way's north, because moss only grows on the north side... Da says so.'

Alex walked back into the woods and stood on a boulder at the edge of the path. 'But this one's covered in moss,' he said.

'Well... that's because it's in the shade.'

'It's a good-for-nothing boulder then. Doesnae speak to anybody. It's in a huff.'

Forbes squinted, then smiled.

Alex guessed they must be alike. People said so. Two peas in a pod. Three if you counted their dead brother, Peter. The same freckly faces, brown eyes and brown hair, only Alex's was cropped to a quarter of an inch and Forbes's was a bushy mess. Apart from that, you could tell Forbes was Forbes, because he had a squint, a lazy eye that Ma said made him handsome and a scar above his lip where he'd caught a twist of fencepost wire and sometimes his neck twitched.

After exploring the pine forest, they made their way by the farmhouse down to Corkerhill village on the other side of Hardridge.

Coggie was with two boys in the field outside the shop.

'Hey!' one of them shouted. 'Kick it over.'

Their ball was on the road.

Forbes ran and leaned back as if to kick it high, then stopped and toed it gently. A half-brick spilled out. 'Aye. Right! We're no falling for that.' He threw the burst ball at them.

'Don't get your knickers in a twist, Forbes. We're only having a laugh,' said the lanky boy, Jamie Bryce.

'Alright Jamie,' Alex said.

'Alright mate,' Jamie replied. He'd taken a stretch, his hair had grown long, but his bony face hadn't changed — lumpy cheekbones like a boxer's, a bottom lip like a toddler in a huff and a stubby nose that rode up his face when he talked.

The wee boy next to him was McPeat, skinny with ears that looked as if they'd been ironed flat to his head, wide eyes, and hair hard to the scalp, like Alex's. He was in shorts, at least two sizes too big, and holey sandshoes, his ribs stuck out on his bare chest and his left eye was bruised.

Nearby, a pack of dogs were bouncing around and getting closer, Homeless among them, pinning the younger dogs that got in its way.

'Here boy. C'mon boy!' Coggie shouted. 'Show me your happy tail.'

Homeless came to her, his head low and tail wagging.

'I wouldnae get too friendly with that mutt if I was you,' Jamie said.

Coggie put her arms around the dog's thick neck. 'He's only a big teddy. Come and cuddle him.'

'That'll be right. It's a fleabag.'

Coggie scrunched her face at Jamie and covered the dog's ears with her hands. 'Don't listen to him, Homeless.'

'It howls at the moon. It's bonkers. Should be put to sleep... put out its misery.'

'Shut it Bryce or I'll set him on you. It's you that should be put to sleep. You talk too much. It's that big gob of yours... you could fit a coconut in that gob, sideways.'

Jamie laughed. 'I don't like coconuts.' He bent down and ruffled the dog's head. 'Only kidding, mate,' he said to it.

McPeat tapped Alex's shoulder. 'We're gonni go hang a swing at the river. Want to go?'

Alex looked to Forbes.

'Aye, we'll go,' Forbes said.

They set off along the terraces, passing houses that looked like they'd come from toy town — redbrick walls, stepped-up gable ends with sandstone balls on top, and fancy black iron palings on balconies that overlooked long gardens down to the railway.

Coming off the path at the end of the terrace, they squeezed through a hole in the fence, the kids and the dogs, onto the lines.

There were lots of lines, shiny ones on the two main tracks, others that went in and around the maintenance sheds and rusty ones at the sides. McPeat walked ahead, on his toes, swinging his arms and singing a tune from *The Jungle Book*.

'That's it!' Jamie said. 'That's who you are. You're Blue the Bear from now on. The bear from the film, get it? That's your nickname.'

'Naw it isnae,' McPeat said, stopping and shaking his head. 'It isnae the bear that sings that song, it's the ape. Anyhow it's Baloo the Bear, no Blue the Bear.'

'Who gave you the keeker?' Alex asked.

McPeat put his hand over his bruise. 'My old man. I got blamed for setting the middens on fire. My old dear telt him no to hit me on the face but that big smelly stinking bastard just goes and does it.'

They passed a diesel train that was having its tank filled. There was no one taking care of the hose and the oil was overflowing and seeping under a patch of blackened cobbles. Further along, a queue of steam engines stood dark and silent outside the sheds.

'They're for the scrapheap,' Jamie said. 'It's their last trip.'

The track led to a lopsided hut on a turntable platform. Approaching it, the dogs went sniffing left and right with their noses to the ground, and when the boys bounced stones off the roof, cats came diving through a hole in the side and scattered in all directions. The dogs flew at them, in a charge of high-pitched yelping that sounded in the bushes, in the sheds, and in the gardens on the Mosspark side of the lines.

Jamie booted the door open to a choking waft of paraffin and cat's pee. Inside, dust floated in sunbeams that shone through holes in the timbers, and at least two leftover cats hissed from the shadows. Only Forbes was brave enough. He stomped in and came out dragging a thick oily rope that he coiled round his shoulder with the help of Coggie and McPeat.

The big cranking wheel on the turntable was just asking to be turned. After daring themselves, they began turning it, making the platform creak and clank and shift out of line with the oncoming track — a racket that alerted the railway worker who shouted a warning from the sheds.

'The polis are here!'

They got off their marks, bolting across the ash flats. It wouldn't have done Alex much use if anyone was really after them. His throat burned at the sudden effort and his legs quickly wanted to pack in.

The others waited at the fence of railway sleepers on the edge of the woods and then made their way along the path. Drawn by a babble of voices, they came to a cycle track that was marked-out around abandoned bits of train, burnt cars and silver birch trees that grew here and there in the ash. Older boys were racing round it on makeshift bikes, their wheel spokes glinting through storms of dust and grit as they skidded past.

On the second lap, a front wheel touched a back wheel, sending both cyclists crashing to the ground. One of them, a fat-faced stocky boy in denim shorts and army boots, picked up his bike and held it over his head and chucked it aside. He limped towards the giggling kids, stopped in front of Alex and pointed to his cut knee. Black ash had mixed with the blood trickling down his shin.

'Lick it!' he said.

'Lick it yourself.'

The boy dabbed the wound with the heel of his hand and wiped the blood on Alex's T-shirt. 'Lick it!'

Coggie squeezed between them, facing the boy with her chin up and her hands in the back pockets of her jeans. 'Beat it, Grogan, ya clatty slob.'

Alex liked the way she spoke. There was no fear.

Grogan looked around. Forbes had ditched the rope and was holding a stick like a baseball bat, and Jamie had stepped in close.

'What? Youse don't think I want to hang around with a bunch of spoon lickers, eh?'

'Take a gander at yourself Grog-on,' Jamie said.

Alex laughed at that.

Grogan jabbed him in the chest. 'You're getting weighed–in, baldy.'

'Aye, you and who else, fat-face,' Forbes said.

Grogan was already walking away. 'We'll see.'

The trek to the river took them up and down mounds of earth and fallen branches, over gullies of oily stream water, zigzagging past snagging brambles and stinging ivy. At a fallen sycamore, they stopped to climb it. Its root ball was sticking up in the air and its sloping trunk was covered in ferns and moss and hanging ivy. A massive chestnut tree was keeping it from falling flat. They sat on the trunk, taking a breather in the stifling heat of the forest.

'Got to watch that nutter, Phil Grogan,' McPeat said. 'He's a flaky-taker. Got a slate loose, so he has. Got expelled for chucking a chair at a teacher. You cannae fight him.'

'Who cannae?' said Forbes.

'You don't know that mob. You don't want to fall out with any of them bampots.'

The riverside, where they got to it, was steep and surrounded by giant hogweed, so they walked alongside until the purple flowering plants took over and the bank sloped easily to the water's edge. A rope swing was already in place, tied to an overhanging branch of an oak tree. Alex shielded his eyes to get an idea of the depth but could not see beyond the reflection of sky and trees and the glistening blue, green and yellow traces of diesel oil being dragged slowly downstream.

The sun, the heat and the water acted on them. The boys stripped to their shorts, Coggie kicked off her shoes and socks and they each took hold of the rope and ran along the bank until it tightened and lifted them in an arc high over the river. They let go, yelling as they dive-bombed into the deep cold water. It shocked them breathless. Half-panicking, they doggy-paddled giggling and spluttering to the opposite bank, climbed onto the golf course they lay on their backs to catch their breath, letting the sun take away the chill.

McPeat turned on to his front. 'Wow, I'd like to see that go up,' he said.

The others turned and saw what he saw. Not far along the river was a sunlit building, some sort of stately mansion, standing proud on the landscape like a massive fort.

'Get a grip,' Forbes said, thumping him on the arm.

McPeat smiled as if he might have been serious or just kidding.

'I've heard it's a museum. You're allowed to go inside and look around.' Jamie said, edging up close to Alex. 'We can go suss it. See what's for snaffling and that. Only me and you, mind. Don't go telling naebody, right?'

'Aye, sure.'

Golfers appeared on the fairway, so they jumped back in the river and played at the rope swing until the sun dipped and the cool evening air made them shiver. They set off for the housing scheme, crossing the fields ahead of their long stretching shadows, their skin tingling from sunburn and scratches.

This new place was amazing. There was no one stopping you from going as far as you wanted. Alex couldn't wait to be back out again and was already planning a trip to the mansion with Jamie.

At home, he went straight to the kitchen, turned on the tap and leaned over the enamel sink to gulp from the cold flowing water, followed by Forbes. They burped and giggled.

Ma was still in her night coat, looking pale and tired. She didn't ask where they'd been all day, who they'd been with and what they'd been doing. Da's only complaint was that their dinner had gone hard in the oven. They were to be back by six from now on.

Crates

On hearing Jamie whistle, Alex picked out a scrap of bacon from the frying pan and made his way downstairs. He stepped into the back garden with Homeless at his side. The dog stuck close to him, nuzzling his hip as he walked around in circles.

Jamie was doing keepie-ups with a manky old ball. He put his foot on it. 'How did you teach him that?' he said, a baffled look on his face.

Alex took the bacon from his pocket and fed it to the dog. 'Clever, eh?'

'Ha ha, that's cheating.'

'It works. He likes me now.'

'Don't start trusting that thing. I'm telling you, mate.'

The woman from the ground-floor flat, Missus Little, came through the close to peg up her washing. 'Hop it the pair of you,' she ordered, placing her basket at her feet. 'You've no right in here with that ball dirtying the laundry and that dog shitting all over the place.'

The boys shared a glance and giggled.

'You won't think it's funny if I go and have a wee word with your dads.'

'Neither will you... mine's been dead for years!' Jamie said and laughed.

She flapped an arm at him. 'Away you go.'

The dog stayed with them as far as the fence on the Haggs Castle golf course, and after they belly-vaulted over the top, it clawed the ground and threw itself against the mesh, howling and barking.

'See you later, Homeless,' Alex said.

'That's a daft name for a mad beast like that. It should be Rip or Fighter or Tank, something hard.'

'So you wouldnae call it Toots?'

'Toots. That'd be something. Or Lollipop. Can you imagine it?'

The hot weather wasn't for letting up, not a cloud in the sky as they sauntered across the fairways, over a slatted timber bridge and into a field of black and white cows that were hunkered down, minding their own business. At the river, they stopped to skip stones across the top of a foaming waterfall and when they moved on, a few steps beyond the trees, they were standing on a dirt road below the big mansion.

Behind its garden walls, flowers surrounded bowling-green lawns and climbing plants dripped from terraces, summerhouses and staircases.

A whirring engine turned their heads. To their left, inching its way round a bend, was a gleaming single-decker bus, out of place in the park, scraping against trees and snapping branches. They followed it to a courtyard where passengers got off, speaking American like on telly, in their bright clothes, hats and cameras, and posing for photos before shuffling into the mansion.

The sign said, *Now Open to the Public.*

A man in a chair at the other side of the doorway was reading the Daily Record. From behind it he warned the boys, 'Touch anything and I'll kick your arses.'

The place was so grand that Alex immediately felt as if he had no right being there. Everything shone — the marble staircases, the polished mahogany banisters, the statues, the glossy paintings and the massive lantern that hung in the centre of the ceiling.

Another man, same bottle green uniform, was on the balcony between the two marble staircases, talking to the Americans... 'Sir John Stirling Maxwell's family were prominent in this area for over seven hundred years. In 1966, they donated the house and the park, hundreds of acres of it, to the City. Here on my right you'll see an astronomical clock with the family coat of arms engraved on the face dating back to 1764. It still works like new, by the way.'

Nodding and smiling, the Americans clicked their cameras as they went from room to room while he waffled on about everything — the furniture, the pillars, the frog-eyed portraits that were nowhere near as good as Nathan's, the grand piano, the ornaments. He even had a story about the wallpaper.

'He's doing my nut in,' Jamie said. 'Let's see what's for taking.'

That's what boys do, Alex told himself, they nick stuff and boast about it. Still, they'd be in deep shit if they got caught nicking anything from this palace.

The guide gestured to a painting of a woman that hung above one of the fireplaces in the library. 'Let me introduce *The Lady in a Fur Wrap,* painted in 1577 by El Greco. No one is sure who she is, although you can tell from her rich clothing, her silk veil and gemstone rings, that she's someone special, well-off for the times... it's a masterpiece that's been displayed at galleries across Europe, envied by art collectors everywhere.' He pointed to a painting above the other fireplace. 'That one there, *Portrait of a Man*, is also an El Greco.'

'Was that his nickname?' asked Alex.

From the scowl on the guide's face, you'd have thought Alex had just interrupted some sort of sacred ritual.

'Good question, young man,' said one of the American ladies.

The guide changed his expression and said, 'That is a good question, son. El Greco means The Greek. It's much easier to say than his real name, Domenikos Theotokopoulos.' He laughed at his own joke, then ushered the tourists to the next room, hanging back to have a word with Alex and Jamie. 'Fuck off you two,' he hissed.

'That's us been telt then,' Jamie replied.

As they waited for the group to move on, it seemed as if the woman in the painting was staring, drawing Alex's attention.

27

Her dark sparkling eyes were nothing like the bulging eyes on the other paintings and her soft stare reminded him of his mother's stare, the one just before she put on her funny face, raising an eyebrow and lowering the other.

'You done gawping?' Jamie said, opening the lid on a writing bureau.

'Pack it in. There's nowt we can nick in here.'

'What d'you mean? There's loads.'

'I mean there's too many people around.'

That didn't stop Jamie. He slid out drawers and opened more lids, then spotted silver plates in a cabinet through the open doorway of a side room. 'See! They're worth decent money. A right few quid, dead or alive.'

'Eh?'

'Melted for scrap or sold as seen.'

Hurrying for a closer look they almost bumped into another uniformed worker, a white-haired man who was swigging on a hipflask. He plugged it and tucked it in his pocket and wiped his chin with the back of his hand. 'I thought I heard bright young voices,' he said. 'I took you as part of the tour party.'

Jamie put on an act, 'It's pure brilliant, mister, being allowed to see these things from yonks ago and that.'

'I like that big clock,' Alex added.

'Interested in history? Well, I'm glad to hear it. Young folk usually don't care.' He held out his hand and gave a cheery grin. 'Iain Mackenzie, Chief Archivist.'

No one had asked Alex to shake hands before, never mind an adult. He did it quickly and Jamie did the same. The man put his arms around their shoulders and said, 'I think I can show you a wee bit of history that'll interest you,' leading them to the hall and down the staircase.

They were walking faster than he was, wriggling free, when he called out to the guard at the door. 'Hey, Bill, I'm taking these two young gentlemen to see a few of the Burrell pieces.'

The guard lowered the newspaper. 'Watch it lads, old Mackenzie there can talk the ears off a donkey.'

The boys relaxed at that and allowed Mackenzie to show the way to the basement.

At the foot of the stairs he hauled an iron gate along its runners. It squeaked and folded up like a concertina, taking them into a long corridor. He introduced the doors as they passed. 'The linen room, the dry goods store, the servants' hall, the gun room, the butlers' room, the pressing room and the house kitchen... the servants earned their keep down here.' He turned the latch on the door at the end of the corridor and stepped across a hallway to a darkened storeroom. Wooden crates, stacked two and three high, blocked the light from a small window high on the wall.

Mackenzie switched on a desk lamp and beckoned to the boys. 'Come and have a peek. I bet you've never seen writing like this.' He opened a thick leather-backed book and tapped it with his fingers. 'It's my job to record every artefact owned by Glasgow Corporation. Thousands of entries in here, all scrolled with pen and ink, all my own handiwork. Not one correction.'

'You need a steady hand for that job, mister,' Jamie said.

'A steady hand and a lot of skill. The way things should be done, not the way they want to do it now that they've got this place to manage, as well as the Burrell.'

'What's the Burrell?'

'The Burrell Collection... they want me to jot it down in scribbles so that wee lassies can type it up for microfilming. Wee lassies and machines taking men's jobs. It just isn't right.'

'Collection of what?'

Mackenzie leaned back on a crate to light up the stump of a cigarette. 'Sir Willie Burrell was a wealthy businessman who owned cargo ships and gathered treasures from all over the world. You could say he had a fancy for fancy things. If it glimmered, he grabbed it. He collected until he got old and then gifted it to Glasgow Corporation. That was thirty-odd years ago, yet it's been stowed away in dusty hideouts ever since.'

'How did this Sir Willie guy get them?'

'People in these far-flung countries wouldn't have seen any worth in them. Sold them for next to nothing. A few bags of rice, likely.'

'He conned them?'

'Well, maybe not him, but someone got a bargain. Let's just say no one at City Chambers is volunteering to hand them back. There's talk of a new museum to show it off. If only the big wigs could get their act together. There's been no control. Councillors have got pieces in their offices — precious Egyptian, Islamic, Chinese and Japanese artefacts. I've heard it's even in their living rooms. It's a scandal. Sir Willie must be turning in his grave.'

'Can we see inside?' Jamie asked, pointing to the crates.

Mackenzie ran his finger down the page. 'Patience, boy, is a virtue.' He wrote a number on the back of a cigarette packet and then squeezed his way around the packing crates, all marked *'Fragile. Handle with Care.'* He used a jemmy to open one, rummaged through the straw inside and fished out a metal hat. For a moment he stood dead still, staring at it like it was magical.

'This helmet belonged to a warrior from two thousand years ago. It's bronze. Here, feel the weight.'

Alex took it and shifted it in his hands, searching for hints why that battered old piece of metal was so special. When he moved to try it for size, Mackenzie grabbed it back. 'It's not a toy.'

'Got any suits of armour?' Jamie asked.

'All the big pieces are either in the Kelvin Hall or the Art Gallery... although there's some interesting armoury I could let you see.' With the cigarette between his teeth, he jemmied another lid and lifted out a varnished wooden case. 'Wait till you feast your eyes on this,' he said, swivelling the latches. 'You're now looking at a snap pistol used by the Jacobites in the 1745 uprising.' He lifted it carefully, both hands, and passed it to Jamie.

'Jacobites rule!' Jamie said, levelling it at Alex's head.

Mackenzie swiped it from him. 'Give me strength! These are historical artefacts.' He put it back in its case and placed it under the straw, then frowned, muttering to himself as he removed a small blue dish. 'What's happened? A Chinese incense bowl. It shouldn't be. I've already logged and labelled one of these, and now I find its twin hiding from me. There's no record of a pair. Even if there was, it's not meant to be with the armoury.'

Alex and Jamie shrugged at each other.

'Let me think. Do I alter the ledger or make a new entry? I need to figure this out.'

Jamie jerked his chin towards the packing crates at the back of the room, giving Alex the signal. Alex's job was to keep Mackenzie busy. He couldn't back down and let Jamie think he wasn't up to it.

'What's a Jacobite?'

'It's not my fault. These records were meant to be meticulous. Spot on, I was told, yet every bloody time... errors and omissions everywhere.'

'I was asking about the Jacobites, Mister Mackenzie. The pistol and that.'

'Jacobites. Right,' Mackenzie said, turning his back for a moment to sup from the hipflask. 'There's a story and a half. You might be surprised to learn that people who owned mansions like this fought with the English against the Jacobite clans.'

Jamie was back at Alex's side. Not likely he had enough time to nick anything. Alex began to take an interest in the story.

'The thing is...' Mackenzie said, flicking cigarette ash into the palm of his hand. 'Got to watch I don't start a fire... the thing is, most of the Scottish landowners were gifted their big country estates and fancy titles as a reward for helping to crush the clans.'

'Rotten bastards,' Alex said.

'The English banned the bagpipes and the kilt after the battle of Culloden.'

'Thank God for that. You'll no catch me wearing a skirt,' Jamie said.

'They built Fort George in the highlands and they've been here ever since with their—'

Jamie butted in. 'We need to get going, it's getting near my dinner time. My granny'll be raging if I'm late. Do you know what'll happen?'

'No. What?'

'I'll need to eat it cold,' Jamie replied, and smiled.

'Oh, well. Better be on your way. Bill will be shuttering-up soon anyhow.'

Bill was still in the chair as they made their way outside. 'I hope they huvnae got the crown jewels stuffed up their jumpers,' he said.

Mackenzie put his arms round both boys and squeezed them in close. 'They're good lads, welcome back anytime.'

Once outside, Jamie wanted to cross a field of Highland cows to a bank of trees. He was wringing his hands and cracking his knuckles.

'You must be kidding. They've all got horns. Why that way anyhow?'

Jamie moved to the ferns and squatted behind the high stems. 'Have a gander, mate,' he said. He was holding an ornament of a Chinese man with a long white beard and a glossy emerald-green coat.

Alex squatted next to him. 'Christsake! I didnae see you. I didnae think you took anything.'

'Got to take your chances, mate. My old man used to blag something every time he went into a shop, but I'll bet he never blagged anything like this. It's pure porcelain. We could be quids-in,' Jamie said, proud of himself. He tucked it inside his waistband and shoved Alex with his open hand, knocking him off balance. 'Ha ha.'

'What'll we do with it?'

'Pawn it or get Danny Toohill to flog it for us. He can flog anything. He's got contacts in the pubs on Paisley Road West.'

'That Mackenzie's a bit of an oddball sure he is?'

'A right fuckin weirdo. But it wouldnae stop me going back for more. First, we need to see how much this fetches. We'll hide it for now in case anybody's after us.'

'Who's after us?'

'Naebody.'

'Then what did you say it for?'

'You cannae be too careful, mate. That's all I'm saying.'

'Where'll we hide it?'

'Bury it somewhere.'

'For how long?'

'Dunno. Couple of weeks at least. Just in case.'

'What about under the turntable?'

'Aye, let's check it out.'

Back in the woods they stuck to the path and came out at the ash flats. They reached the turntable unnoticed, dropped to the pit and dragged themselves underneath, into a space boxed-off by riveted steel plates, girders, wheels and windings. It was cool and quiet, and they could see the sky passing through spaces in the sleepers above their heads.

Jamie swept away a spider's web and carefully placed the ornament inside the channel of a girder. 'You'll be safe in there, Wee China,' he said to it.

Means Test and Binnie

The means tester man came to the house because Da had applied for a clothing grant on top of the free school meals. He ogle-eyed everything, making Alex take notice of the damp stains, the bare window, the bare light bulb dangling from its wire, worn lino, and him and Forbes sitting on the couch with their shoes coming apart and their clothes torn.

'Did you dress them like that for my benefit?' the man asked, fidgeting with his collar to free his wrinkled neck.

Da stood holding baby Sarah. 'It's all they've got. I cannae send them to school like that.'

'You need to demonstrate eligibility for these benefits. Are you still unemployed?'

'That's right.'

'Three children at home?'

'Right.'

'This housing scheme's been set aside for skilled tradesmen, so I'm finding it difficult to understand why you haven't found work. You have got a trade?'

'Aye.'

'Doing what?'

'Landscaping, drainage and the like.'

'There's lots of that kind of work around.'

'If there is, I cannae find it. I've walked to the East End and back. It's no easy finding decent work unless you know the handshake.'

'You should be taking on any kind of work. How much do you have in the bank?'

'Down to my last couple of hundred thousand.'

'I've heard them all before, Mr Hannah. You need to answer my questions. I take it you're fit?'

'Aye. I'm no claiming sick.'

'When did your employment end?'

'August last year.'

'Where was that?'

'All over. Water Board work.'

'Reason for leaving?'

'To take care of my wife. She's sick in bed… we lost our oldest, you see.'

The man followed Da's glance to the photo of Peter. It was the one they took of him at school in front of a painted curtain that was supposed to be sky. Back in the Gorbals, when they'd kept him in hospital, Ma had lit candles next to it, and prayed and cried over it. She never missed going to see him, taking him presents like it was non-stop birthdays. None of it worked. Maybe it was why she didn't do the same for Alex.

The man coughed to clear his throat. 'They'll each get two outfits... and winter jackets.'

He jotted down the boys' names, ages and shoe sizes, tore off a slip and handed it to Da. 'The address is on the back. Do you know how to get there?'

'I know it.'

'I'm sorry. It must be devastating to lose a child.'

After the man left, Forbes sat with his arms folded, refusing to budge. 'People are gonni laugh at us. McPeat wears corpie handouts and everybody calls him a pauper. I'm no wearing it. I'm gonni get a paper round so I am. Buy my own clothes.'

'Don't make this any harder than it is, son.'

Alex didn't start school with the other kids at the end of the summer break. A letter had arrived, saying he needed a doctor's note clearing him. It took days to sort out. Then, on the night before he was due to start, he couldn't sleep.

'I'll look a right daftie, the new boy in corpie gear.' In his mind, he was talking to Peter.

'You'll get slagged rotten.'

'And there's the polis to worry about. They might turn up looking for the boys who stole from the mansion.'

'Could get put in a home.'

'It isnae really stealing if it was knocked off in the first place, is it?'

'Fair's fair.'

'It deserved to be nicked. I promise, if it gets sold, I'll give the money to Ma.'

'You won't keep it?'

'Nah, not all of it.'

He was still awake when the diesel engines started on the nightshift at the railway sheds. The hum drifted over the fields, along the streets and through the skinny windowpanes, a droning rise and fall. The rhythm of it slowed his mind.

Up at six, he got dressed in his too-small clothes and decided to put up with the old jumper even though the sleeves were well shy of his wrists, but not the half-mast trousers. He put on the corpie ones instead. They didn't look so bad. The coarse black jacket was for the cold weather, so he wouldn't need to worry about that for a while.

He waited by the window for Homeless to bark at the milk float, three quick ones, a pause, and then a long growling one, like always. When he heard it, he lifted the scraps he'd set aside from dinner and took them downstairs. The dog went mental for them, twisting this way and that, sending slobbers all over the place.

It was half-eight and spitting rain by the time he and Forbes left the house. They split on the main road, Forbes walking with the ranks of primary kids making their way towards Pollok, Alex towards the secondary school in Cardonald. Seeing Coggie up ahead, he hurried to catch her. She took him on a shortcut through the construction site for the new college, and when they reached school, she showed him to the office.

The office woman read the doctor's note, searched her files for ages, and then told him to report to Miss Binnie, 1B Boys, on the ground floor.

'I'm meant to be in second year.'

'First year, 1B, off you go.'

'But I'm fourteen. I'm meant to be in second year.'

'No one goes straight from primary to second year.'

'I got lessons in hospital.'

'I'll see if it can be fixed. Off you go for now. First right, last door on left.'

Alex walked into the class and stood, all eyes on him, waiting for the teacher to notice. The kids were set up like in primary school, big ones at the back and small ones at the front. McPeat was in the second row, behind the Toohill twins from the biggest tribe in Hardridge. He recognised nobody else.

The teacher kept on with the register, calling out names and getting mumbled replies, 'Here Miss.'

'Name, and why are you here?' she said, turning to him at last.

'Alex Hannah. The office woman says I've to report to 1B for now. I've to be in second year.'

She rose looking him up and down through black-rimmed spectacles that curled upwards at her temples. He was taller, even allowing for her bird-nest hair.

'Hands out of pockets, stand up straight, and say "Miss Binnie" when you address me. Understand?'

Alex took his hands from his pockets, straightened up and smiled. 'Yes. Miss Binnie.'

'Take that stupid smirk off your face!'

'Yes... Miss... Binnie.'

McPeat and a few other boys giggled, but her stare quickly put an end to that. 'I'll seat you with the uppers,' she said, walking between the desks to the back of the room. She stood by an empty chair. 'Here.'

As Alex slid into it, a sharp pain shuddered his skull. Binnie had jabbed him with her fingernail.

He rubbed his head furiously. 'What did you need to go and do that for!'

'If you choose to act the clown, carry-on, talk or fidget you'll be sitting next to smelly McSweeney where I can keep a close watch on you.'

The lines of stares met at the small boy in the desk nearest to the door.

At morning break, Alex buddied-up with McPeat, sheltering in the toilets where boys hung around in groups, smoking and gambling for pennies. Others didn't mind the rain and played football. There were no girls, they had their own classes and their own playground at the other side of the building.

'That was a belter she hit me. It's still stinging.'

'She's got iron fingers.'

'She hates me already.'

'She's either all sugar or all shite. Mostly all shite. We've got to put up with that old hag for twelve periods a week.'

McPeat knew all about her. He was repeating first year to catch up with the lessons.

'How come she calls McSweeney smelly?'

'On the first day back, she goes sniffing round the classroom, saying she can smell something wiffy. She goes to McSweeney and asks if he'd peed himself. McSweeney says his wee brother must've peed the bed and the pee must've gone on his vest and dried in. Binnie makes him take it off in front of the whole class. She holds it up with her pencil and there's a big yellow tidemark like a map of Africa. She sprays her purple perfume everywhere and says she's disgusted. She's got a cheek... her perfume's worse than the pissy smell. It gives you the boak, so it does.'

By the end of the week, Binnie had appointed McPeat as Class Prefect. She told him it was because of his special knowledge of the school. She gave him a badge and asked what he thought of having such an important job.

His answer caused a wave of giggles. 'My tummy feels a bit shitey, Miss.'

'I beg your pardon?'

McPeat rubbed his stomach. 'My tummy, you know—'

'You mean you feel a bit nervous?'

'Aye, that's right Miss, shitey.'

Because Alex was laughing when no one else was, she dragged him from his chair and sat him in the front row. 'I'll bang your head off the wall if I have to!'

He tried to pay attention after that but found it difficult. She droned on and on, repeating things in her half-chanting voice, boring stuff, the same every day, and crap religious stories too, about kings of Babylon and firstborn sons. Her English lessons were even worse. Reading practice went clockwise round the desks with each boy stumbling through a page. Alex began counting the pages against the number of boys before him, finding the page he'd be asked to read. He rehearsed it in his head, and when his turn came, he read it out smoothly, then relaxed as the session went on. He soon drifted away on a daydream, a habit he'd mastered in hospital.

The image of the painting in the mansion house jumped to mind. When he imagined it, he saw his mother, happy and thoughtful, the way she used to be. It made him to think of the story that Nathan had told — the one about the Italian guy going to a museum and walking out in broad daylight with the *Mona Lisa* under his arm. Nathan was right, it was pretty cool. And if the geeky *Mona Lisa* was worth a million, how much was the *Lady in a Fur Wrap* worth? His mind played a scene where he showed it to his mother and it delighted her, putting a stop to her low moods. It'd be dead easy to take it from the wall.

'Read on from there, Hannah.'

He'd sneak it past the guard.

'Hannah!'

A wooden duster struck the wall next to him and skittered along the tiled floor. Binnie had doubled back, changing the routine to catch him out.

'Missed,' he said.

She took the belt from the drawer and whacked it off his desk. 'Go stand in the corridor until I'm good and ready to deal with you!'

He wasn't for hanging around until she was good and ready to deal with him. He walked out and went to find Jamie.

Connected

They sat cross-legged under the turntable, facing each other and staring at the ornament on the ground in front of them.

Jamie cracked his knuckles. 'We could be talking a fiver, a tenner, a ton. To be honest, mate, I huvnae got a clue. But see when you think about it, being in the crates with all them other fancy things… what did Mackenzie call them?'

'Artefacts.'

'Aye, they don't come cheap. Cost a packet them artefacts.'

'But it doesnae look like much, does it?'

'Best if we go see Danny Toohill. I've already telt him about it. He'll be at the Grogans' hoose playing cards.'

'You're kidding!'

'Don't worry, fat-face won't be there. His old man kicks him out to school before he leaves for work. Should be in the loony school, that halfwit.'

'Is Danny Toohill okay? Do you trust him?'

'That's what he's for. He gets shot of stuff.'

'I'll tell you who we need,' Alex said. 'We need that master thief from the program on telly. What's he called in it? He steals diamonds and gets hunted by this woman who's like Miss World, but she's really a detective and she disnae know he's really a spy. If we've tanned a pure valuable treasure, it might be on the telly and we'll be on the run with Miss World chasing us.'

Jamie toed the sole of Alex's shoe. 'Dream on.'

A girl, about eighteen, answered the door and showed them into the smoke-filled living room. The card school was in full flow. Danny Toohill had won a hand and was using his cards to scoop in the winnings. He glanced at the boys. 'Look who it is, the heavy team. Pinky and Perky,' he said. 'Fifty pence post, if you want in.'

The gamblers were all men in their late teens or early twenties, all with side-shed hair and sideburns, nylon polo-necked jumpers and denims. They sat with their piles of coins and their cigarettes on the table. The girl, standing, looked on.

Danny slipped a Woodbine from a packet, sparked a Zippo lighter and jerked his head back from the long flame. He lit up carefully, shuffled the pack and dealt two cards to each player, one face down and one face up.

He turned to the boys. 'Let's see it then.'

Jamie took the Wee China from Alex's schoolbag and held it up. 'Worth a pure fortune, so it is. It's got a red stamp with Chinese writing.'

'That'll fetch naff all.'

'Come off it, Danny. It's ancient. Really dear, like a hundred quid.'

'Looks like it's been nicked from somebody's hoose. It isnae youse two who's been tanning the hooses in the street, is it? Somebody's gonni be getting their heads kicked in for that.'

'Of course it isnae us... you interested in this or no?'

'Where did you get it?'

'China.'

'You want a slap?'

A man rapped the table and said, 'Twist.' No doubt Grogan's older brother, the same big round face and stocky build. 'Give you ten bob for it if I win this hand.'

'Swap it for the clock,' said the girl, pointing to an ornament on the window sill — a brown Clydesdale horse with its front legs raised and a small round clock on its backside.

Grogan's brother put his arms round her waist and pulled her close to him. 'That's my mammy's silver wedding present I'll have you know.' He rapped the table again. 'Twist!'

Danny dealt a five on top of the five that was already showing.

'Stick.'

After turning his own hand, a queen and a six, Danny took a third card, an eight. 'Burst for fucksake!'

'How about it?' Jamie said.

Danny shrugged. 'Half a quid's a fair offer I'd take it if I were you.'

'It's a done deal,' said Grogan's brother, holding out fifty pence. 'Here, take it and give us the goods.'

'No way. It's worth stacks.'

Alex grabbed the Wee China and stuck it back in the bag, making it clear that they weren't about to haggle on that joke offer. They left quickly.

They caught a bus on Mosspark Boulevard, got off at Shawlands Cross and walked along Queen's Park to the pawnshop.

'Let me do the talking this time,' Jamie said. 'I know the owner.'

'How come?'

'I'm connected y'know.'

'Aye, right.'

'You wouldnae believe me if I telt you.'

'You're gonni tell me anyhow.'

'My granny took me to the pawn when we lived in the Gorbals, but no for pawning nowt.'

'Naw? What else would you go to the pawn for?'

'Family business. See, she'd been taking care of this old guy, Imrie, and his son. The son's in a wheelchair and cannae do nowt for himself, then the old guy takes sick and it's a sorry state. By this time, the demolition's getting started, and we're the last two families in the street, them at one end, us at the other. Everybody else had flitted. Nae streetlights or nothing. I helped. I went there after school and took turns of feeding the son, I'm talking spoon-feeding here, but I wouldnae empty the old guy's piss bucket. My granny did that. She got him medicine, cooked and cleaned and that... anyhow, the old guy gets worse, so she goes searching their flat for an address book or a letter or something, saying they must have kin. At first, she cannae find nothing. She sits on the couch thinking, gets up and goes straight to the scullery. And there it is, stuck inside a tin of baking soda — a passport with a photo of Imrie, only that isnae his name. It's Immerman. And the photo's stamped with the Star of David.'

'So what?'

'It means he's Jewish.'

'So what?'

'It means we go to the pawn, my granny and me. She sees Melville Samuels, the owner, and tells him that one of his kin needs help. And that was that.'

'That was what?'

'The next day a big flashy limo comes to the Gorbals and takes away Imrie and his son. Couple of days later me and my granny gets invited to a big posh hoose for a nosh-up, a reward for taking care of the Imries. A few days after that and we get a letter from the corpie saying we're flitting to Hardridge. The Jewish boss-man arranged it. So that's what I'm telling you. It's about having connections. A wee favour here, a wee turn there.'

As they waited for the pawnbroker to serve his customers, Alex took in the displays: jewellery, lighters, war medals, watches, mantel clocks, cameras, binoculars, stamp collections, musical instruments and more. Pawning seemed like big business. A swaying drunk pawned a bag of joinery tools for loose change. Next, a woman, well-off going by her appearance, laid a coat on the counter and stroked it, saying it was genuine leopard-skin, almost new. She had a receipt for ninety-nine quid, yet she was only asking for fifteen, enough to tide her over until her husband returned home from the merchant navy. She accepted five and hurried away stuffing the money in her purse. The next customer wanted to buy back her diamond engagement ring. The ticket had expired, meaning she'd have to cough up full price. She'd pawned it for ten, and it was on sale for fifty-five. She called the pawnbroker a money-grabbing weasel, worse than the moneylenders, before storming out and slamming the door.

'Alright Melville,' Jamie said, stepping up to the counter. 'Another happy customer, eh?'

Melville hung the fur coat on a rack. He was older than fifty, sixty maybe, hefty with wavy greying hair and gold-rimmed spectacles. He looked miffed at being called a money-grabbing weasel. 'They're all the same,' he said. 'There's always a sob story. They only need the cash to tide themselves over... until they get themselves sorted. But most of them never do. Gamblers and alkies who'd pawn their granny's glass eye for a few pennies.'

Alex thought about asking after Imrie and his son then decided against it. Jamie could've been making it up.

Jamie put the ornament on the counter, stood back and pointed at it with his hands shaped like pistols. 'What do you think of this Wee China?'

'What is it?'

'It's pure valuable. It's got Chinese writing.'

Melville shrugged as if to say, 'Big deal.' He took a magnifying glass from a shelf, examined the writing on the base and ran a finger over the surface. 'It's rough. Probably cheap clay.'

'You wouldnae call it cheap if you knew where it came from,' Alex said.

Melville looked at him, then turned back to Jamie.

'Don't worry, he's sound,' Jamie said.

'Hasn't been advertised on Crimedesk, has it?' Melville grumbled, turning the antique in his hands.

'If it doesnae interest you, we'll take it to the pawn in Govan.'

Still holding it, Melville said, 'I'm being honest with you. This could be some sort of religious piece... see how his palms are being held out skyward? Religious pieces aren't worth much.' He put it down, out of reach of the boys, and then lifted a book, an antiques guide. He turned a few pages. 'I haven't seen anything like this, and I don't think I will in here... I've not got the foggiest. Best I can do is two quid.'

'Come off it, I can tell you're interested,' Jamie said, not about to give in. 'Give us a fiver for now, see what you get for it and we'll go halves on the rest, a ton each.'

Melville was the one smiling now. 'How did you get hold of it?'

'You know the score, Melville. We cannae tell... only that it's from old crates that were last opened donkey's years ago, I'm talking like forty years, so it isnae hot or anything. We can get loads more like it. Even better things.'

'Is that right? Well, I'll give you two quid for now and fifty percent if it makes more than a tenner.'

After splitting the ticket, the pawnbroker gave half to Jamie and used an elastic band to tie the other half to the statuette. He set it on top of a display cabinet and then slid two pounds from his wallet.

The boys talked it over on the bus home. A pound each and more to come felt like a good deal, and since the pawnbroker was dead keen on the antique, it was bound to be worth a lot more.

'You want to go to the mansion the morra?' Jamie said, 'See what else is on offer.'

'Cannae. I need to go back to school. I'm in bother.'

'For what?'

'I done a runner from class.'

'Shouldnae be a problem. Fake a note from your old dear saying you had a dodgy tummy, or a fever, the black plague or something, send it to the teacher and take the rest of the month off.'

Collection Plate

Before putting the groceries in the kitchen cabinet, Da rechecked the price tags. 'It's daylight robbery,' he said. 'They're all at it. They'll take you for your last penny, every one of them. And I've still got the gas and electric meters to feed.' He sat at the table and opened the newspaper at the horseracing page. 'The bookies are worse than the lot of them.'

'What do you gamble for if you cannae afford it?' Alex said.

'There's nae harm in a wee twenty pence accumulator if it's all you've got to lose.'

'Twenty pee? Is that all you've got?'

'It's all I've got to lose. You best remember what it's like being skint. Get yourself a good trade when you leave school and you won't have to worry about money, you'll have nae bother finding a job.'

'Nathan Coghlin's at art school. I could do that.'

'Art? Nae point. It won't put bread on the table. A trade on the building sites, that's what you need if you don't want to wind up like me.'

'But I thought you had a good trade?'

'Digging holes in the blinding rain, sleet and snow, covered in muck into the bargain, does that sound good to you?'

'Maybe I'll get a paper round like Forbes.'

Forbes had gone round the houses touting for customers like he said he would, picking up eight for the Evening Times and four for the Citizen, spread over Hardridge, Mosspark and Pollok. It was nothing compared to the stacked bags of the other newspaper boys, but it was bringing him good pocket money, even enough to take Alex to the movies now and then.

'I had to leave school at thirteen to earn my keep.'

'Don't tell me... you went there in bare feet. Right?' Alex said, teasing his father.

'You better believe it.'

Alex didn't know much about his parents when they were young, only that his mother had worked as a seamstress at a store in town, and his father, much older, had been in the army during the war. Whenever he asked, it was always the same... 'I'll tell you later, son.'

'By the way, Missus Little came to the door when you were out. She'd been speaking to a priest at the chapel. He's coming to the hoose to see Ma.'

The wrinkles sharpened around Da's eyes, a sign he was ready to lose his temper. 'That lot should mind their own bloody business.'

At least he'd calmed down by the time the front door sounded later that evening, three heavy raps. He got up out of his chair to answer it.

'Father Morrell to see Missus Hannah,' said a deep voice. 'I sent a message. She at home?'

'Aye. Come in.'

The priest walked straight through to the living room and plonked himself on the couch as if he'd been there loads of times. He wore a black cloak over his priest's suit, and a funny peaked hat, which he didn't remove. He bumped along the couch making space for Ma. 'Sit yourself down and take the weight off your feet, Missus Hannah. I'm told you were a wee bit poorly.'

Flustered at getting out of bed, Ma tightened her night coat and ran her fingers through her tangled hair.

After babbling on about Ted Heath, the strikes and the rotten weather, the priest asked to speak to Ma alone. He spent a fifteen minutes with her before Da interrupted, dropping a strong hint, 'Alex'll walk you home.'

'Have a tea before you go,' Ma said.

'Something stronger? A wee nip if you have any.'

Da cracked open a half bottle of whisky that he'd stashed away. He tipped the neck over the chipped tumbler, the only glass in the house. 'Say when.'

The priest waited until the tumbler was two-thirds full before raising his hand. He picked it up, sniffed it and downed it in two gulps. From his red face and veiny nose it was clear he liked a bevy.

'Not having one yourself?' he said.

'Never touch it, except on important occasions,' Da replied. He showed the priest to the door.

'Grief takes time... I'll say a special prayer for her at Sunday's mass.'

'Esther,' Da said.

'Esther. Yes. I'll say a special prayer for Esther.'

Alex couldn't work things out with his mother. Sometimes she seemed okay — like the other day when she was sitting with Sarah on her knee, reading nursery rhymes. But sometimes she wasn't — like earlier, when he'd come home from school to find the place stinking of smoke, the milk pan burning and the handle melting and dripping on the lino. Ribbons of black smoke were floating in the air and she was at the table staring into space, doing nothing about it. He had turned off the gas, smothered the flames with a dishcloth and opened the window. Could she not smell it? See it? What was up with her? He was a good boy, she said, as if that had anything to do with anything. Then Da came back from the shops and told Alex to stop worrying, that lots of people forget to turn off the gas now and again. He put the burnt pan in the sink and talked to Ma as if nothing was the matter, telling her that Missus Little had gone and got stained glass windows fitted, imagine spending money like that on a corpie house, blah, blah, blah — small talk that meant nothing. It was Da's way of hiding things.

Out on the street, Alex lagged behind the priest, trying his best to make it look as if they weren't together as they passed Grogan and his mate, Garry Haughton, nicknamed Haw, who were under the lamppost on the corner, leaning on a fence with their hands in their pockets.

'Where are you going with Batman's grandpa?' Haw said. He was taller than Grogan and easy to spot with his bright ginger hair. He began whistling the Batman tune from telly.

'You've got something of ours. Better part with it soon,' Grogan said.

Alex showed them two fingers and walked on.

'You've got to come back this way, ya skinny prick.'

The priest spoke when they reached the chapel house. 'I'll be watching for your face on Sunday. Yours and your brother's. Your father's too.'

'My da's a proddy.'

He waved Alex off with a flick of his wrist.

A flickering light at the chapel window caught Alex's eye as he walked down the steps. He stepped inside, into the spooky silence. A coffin, draped in a white sheet, had been set on trestles at the altar and candles were burning. There must have been an evening service, for the collection plate was full to the brim. He thought of reasons not to help himself and then thought of the priest's beetroot face gulping the whisky. The old alky didn't even know Ma's name, probably didn't care about her and would probably use the plate money for booze.

He was moving the coins around, looking to see if there were any silver ones, when a voice boomed round the empty church. 'God save us! Thieving from the Lord!'

The priest was standing in the doorway.

In a split second, Alex had sidestepped him and was outside running. He felt the voice chasing him along the dark road, overtaking him, going through the walls of the houses, telling everyone what he'd done. It was the only thing on his mind when Grogan and Haw jumped out of the shadows under the stairs.

Grogan held him in a neck lock and Haw kneed him on the thigh, again and again, giving him a dead leg.

'Where is it?'

'Where's what?' Alex croaked, struggling to breathe.

'The thing that you and Bryce flogged to my brother.'

'We didnae flog it to anybody. We papped it. It wasnae worth a light... a daft brown horse with a clock stuck up its arse.'

'I'll rip you open,' Grogan said through gritted teeth. He let go and pulled a knife from inside his jacket, its long blade clearly visible in the dull glow of the stair light.

With both hands Alex gripped Grogan's wrist.

Grogan spat in his face and clouted him on the ear with his free hand.

'Rattling rosary beads is no gonni help you here. You better part with the Chinaman or it won't be a wee slap next time,' Haw said and pushed Alex away.

After limping upstairs, Alex called out to let his parents know he was home and went straight through to the bedroom. He was lying on the bed when Forbes came in.

'What's the matter?'

'That fat-faced bastard Grogan and his gingernut pal jumped me.'

'What for?'

'For nothing.'

'You hurt?'

'Nah. Gave me a dead leg, that's all.'

'We'll get them back.'

'Forget it.'

Alex closed his eyes, worrying less about the two eejits than he was about the collection plate.

'You praying or something?'

'Resting my eyelids.'

'I'm gonni pray for a bike.'

'You cannae just go and pray for a bike, it's got to be for a good cause,'

'Aye, you can, the priest says so. The Lord always gives you what you ask for. And a bike is a good cause, it helps get you to chapel quick, where you pray for a better bike to get away even quicker.'

Now looking sideways at his brother, Alex said, 'Very funny. You should pray he doesnae come sneaking around here again. Imagine bumping into him during a power cut. You'd cack your pants.'

'Aye, imagine him peeking in your window on a foggy night... lucky we're three up.'

'Guess what happened... he caught me with my hand in the collection plate.'

'When?'

'The night.'

'You're joking.'

'You should've heard him... said I'd stolen God's money. I legged it, but he's bound to tell on me.'

They spoke no more about it until they were having breakfast in the morning when Forbes whispered, 'Say you were putting the money in, no taking it out.'

'Aye, they'll believe me an all.'

'Or go to confession. Then the priest won't be able to say nowt cause it's against the rules.'

'That's a better idea. I'll do that.'

Rocks

Binnie didn't believe the sick note for a second. She scrunched it, chucked it in the bin and dished out six of the belt, bringing it down full force, twisting her lip as she did so. Alex kept his hands high and stared straight at her, unflinching, showing no pain, annoying her even more. It left his hand stinging hot, his wrist bruised purple and his temper raised. He was planning to walk out again. But, just before the period ended, she announced what sounded like excellent luck — she was being promoted to Principal Teacher and wouldn't be taking classes any longer.

'Praise the lord,' McPeat whispered, getting a wave of sniggers and giggles from the boys close enough to hear.

It was even better luck that brought her replacement breezing into the class the following morning, Miss Cleghorn. She seemed far too young to be a teacher, didn't dress like one and didn't teach like one, calling everyone by their first names, and all the time heaping praise on them, making them believe they were being singled out for special attention. At least Alex thought he was. He decided to put up with school for now. There was nothing happening with the Wee China anyway, not yet. It was still at the pawnshop, gathering dust.

Grogan and Haw were the reason he never settled. They began showing up at the school gates with their gang. He carelessly walked into them, got slapped, kicked and spat on. They would keep coming back, they said, until he handed over the ornament. He couldn't be sure when they would turn up. Sometimes they were waiting and sometimes they weren't.

He was sharp out of class every day, but not sharp enough to avoid having to run for his life, so he took to hiding in the toilets, humiliated. He couldn't even risk going out at night in case they were on the prowl, or round the next corner. His only plan was to stay away from them for long enough, hoping they might forget about him and pick on someone else.

They did. They picked on his young brother.

Forbes had gone to collect his bundle of newspapers from the half-four train and wasn't expected back until six but in less than twenty minutes he was hammering on the front door like someone trying to break it down.

His shirt was torn and his arms were scratched and bleeding. Raging and crying, it took him ages to calm down enough to tell Da what had happened. Grogan and his mob had ambushed him at the road bridge. He wouldn't let go his bag of newspapers so they bent back his fingers, kicked his hands, prised it from him and threw it from boy to boy before chucking it in the river. When he fought back, they dragged him by the ankles and dangled him twenty feet above the water.

Da fell silent, his face turning redder and redder. He pulled on his boots and charged downstairs. Alex and Forbes went out to the balcony and watched him marching down the hill.

'Grog-on says you've got something of his. Says you've to hand it over,' Forbes said.

'He's a liar.'

Twenty minutes later and their father came back into view. They ran down to meet him.

'Did you get them?' Forbes asked.

Da kept walking fast towards the house, the boys scurrying behind.

'Did you get them?'

'It's just as well I didnae bloody well get them.'

'You're hopeless,' Forbes bawled. 'Hopeless!'

Alex felt let down too. He wanted his father to grab Grogan by the throat and choke him till his eyes popped. 'They're bastards.'

Da stopped. 'Watch your lip, both of you. You're gonni need to handle it yourself. Fight back or they'll keep picking on you.'

'There's loads of them. We've nae chance.'

'There's two of you. Get hold of one of them, the biggest, and give him a good hiding.'

'Grogan's a mental case and built like a tank,' Alex said.

'Well then, break a clothes pole in half and skud him when he isnae looking.'

'From behind his back?'

'Aye, hard. Knock the shit out of him and his buddies will soon get the message. Now, go back and see if you can find that bag, both of you.'

Down at the river, Alex rescued the dripping bag from among the reeds and tipped the ruined newspapers onto the bank. Forbes was off in a world of his own, making a toy boat from twigs and stems. He launched it and waded out to free it when it snagged on the rocks. Standing knee deep and wobbling on the loose stones on the riverbed, he watched it sail into the darkness under the bridge, then stuck his hand under the water, picked out a fist-sized rock and brought it to the bank. 'Nice and shiny,' he said. 'Good for chucking at them.'

Alex rolled up his sleeve, dropped his hand in the cold water, and lifted out another. He took Forbes's rock and juggled both. 'Good for chucking right enough. Leave it to me.'

'You cannae fight them all.'

'Nah... just one.'

The time and place to fight Grogan was a decision Alex had yet to make, but not outside school. For the next few days, he stuck to the routine of hiding in the toilets. The last thing he expected was to see the gang scaling the fence at lunch break. That's what they did. Six of them came swaggering along the playground towards him.

Boys stopped playing football, fell silent and stood back, creating a wide circle.

He took a rock from his schoolbag and stepped into the open space walking slowly towards them. His heart was thumping against his chest and he was shaking, but not with fear. It couldn't have been fear because he didn't care how it would end. He felt excited, worked up, willing it to happen.

Haw and Grogan glanced at each other, not sure of their next move.

'Couldnae hit a coo's arse with a banjo,' Haw said.

He ducked as Alex threw it.

Grogan didn't duck, and it struck the side of his head. He didn't buckle either. He stood there grinning like an idiot, with dark blood trickling down his face.

Haw was inspecting the wound, admiring it, when the Toohill twins came by Alex's side. Nobody messed with a Toohill. Fight one and you fight the whole tribe. Other boys, offended at the gallus invasion of their school, gathered around Alex. They cheered as the gang scurried back over the fence to the street.

That afternoon, Binnie came to the class, held the door open and yelled, 'Head teacher's office, now!'

Everyone knew who she meant. Alex got out of his chair and followed her along the corridor, planning to speak up for himself. He and Forbes were the ones being bullied.

After being ordered to wait outside the head teacher's office, he put his ear to the door and listened.

'There seems to be an anomaly in your recommendation for remedial class, considering his IQ,' said the head teacher.

'He'd be expelled if it was up to me.'

'Miss Binnie. If we expel every pupil who found themselves in a bit of bother there wouldn't be many for us to teach. We must try to get the best out of them, give them every chance. Now, I'm aware of these thugs hanging around our school, and I want to hear the pupil's account.'

Binnie replied loudly, 'All this new liberal nonsense about making them feel comfortable in class goes against the principles of proper discipline. I've been in education long enough to know that when a child is failing, like he is, it's not the teacher's fault. It's the parents. The boy is trouble. He's been selling his free dinner ticket, upsetting lessons, playing truant, stealing from the collection plate — we know it was him — and now gang fighting. Are we meant to stand back and allow this to happen?'

'Let's hear the pupil's account. Bring him in.'

When he was done listening to Alex, the head teacher looked like he was in two minds as to what to do.

'Right!' he said, slapping the table. 'I'm sending a letter to your parents.'

That sounded okay, Alex thought, waiting for the rest of it.

'You're being reassigned to second year, 2E, alongside boys your own age who won't apply themselves or don't have the academic abilities. Having said that, I'm prepared to offer you a chance. You can use the remainder of this term to convince me that you deserve better, perhaps 2A or 2B. I think you're able, provided you behave and apply a bit of effort.'

Binnie gave a smug look. There was no way Alex was getting out of 2E. If there was a 2Z, he'd be in it. She'd make sure of it.

Payout

Trips to the pawnshop became fewer. Alex didn't mind sneaking away from the crappy woodwork lessons and gym, but he was fed up seeing the Wee China on the shelf. It had been over two months. So when he saw that it was gone, he guessed it had been put aside, in a drawer or a box.

'Hey!' Jamie said, pointing to the space on the shelf.

Melville Samuels came to the counter, took four crispy fivers from his wallet and set them down. 'There you go.'

Jamie pocketed two in his denim jacket and handed two to Alex. 'I telt you in was worth something, sure I did?'

'Just wait to you hear the rest of it.'

'Are the polis sniffing around?'

'No, listen. I knew fine well there was something fishy about the joker who bought it. I should've twigged he was a dealer. I'd seen him in here earlier that afternoon, smartly dressed and carrying a briefcase. Couldn't miss him. I was getting set to lock up for the night when he came back and said he was on a business trip, English accent too, hoping to find a nice gift to take home to his fiancée. Had his eye on the leopard-skin coat, haggled over the price, couldn't be sure if it'd fit, decides he doesn't want to lug it through the airport and lifts his briefcase like he's making to leave. I offer him a few smaller things, nice ring of pearls, selection of earrings. He's huffing and puffing, keeps eyeing his watch, then points to the Chinese ornament. It was all show, the oldest trick in the book — fake interest in something, talk up the purchase, change your mind at the last minute then ask about the thing that you actually want, as if it's an afterthought. This guy knew exactly what he was doing, trying to catch me off-guard. I doubled the price I had in mind and settled for forty-five. My gut told me it could be worth much more. Then again, it had been here for too long without even a sniff of interest. A bird in the hand, I thought, until I read about it in the monthly. The lousy thieving reprobate. A dealer from one of the big auction houses. Someone paid five hundred for it.'

'Five hundred! Are you kidding us?' Jamie said.

'Do I look like I'm kidding? I could've bought a Jag for that money. The thing is... it couldn't have been reported stolen, otherwise the insurance inspectors would've blocked the sale.'

'Can we see this monthly?' Alex asked.

Melville opened a few drawers. 'It's a trade magazine, son. Can't seem to place it right now. I'll put it aside for you if I haven't binned it. You said you can get more like it?'

'Aye,' Jamie replied.

'The storage crates?'

'Aye.'

'Antiques?'

'Loads of Wee Chinas.'

'Bring them in. I'll take them to auction myself.'

'Fifty-fifty?'

'Fifty-fifty.'

'Nae questions?'

'No questions.'

Unsure of what had just happened, Alex tried to weigh it up as they walked home. 'It's like winning the pools then finding out that you forgot to put your coupon on... at least we got ten smackers each, plus the quid we already got. Better than a poke in the eye.'

'Nah. Pawnbrokers are meant to know the score. Him getting conned like that doesnae sound right to me. That story smelt like shite. See if you think about it, you'd need a few grand to buy a Jaguar. Five hundred isnae anywhere near enough. And he's too keen for us to bring him more gear, even though he knows it's knocked off.'

'What are you saying?'

'Could be the Wee China sold for a stack more than he's letting on. He's trying to hide how much. That way he can con us next time. We might need to find a new punter. Maybe Danny Toohill. I telt him about fat-face hounding us. He says if we get anything decent in future, we better not advertise it at the card school. That was a mistake an all.'

They headed down to the railway and walked the track, stepping aside as a freight train came rumbling towards them. It shook the ground at their feet.

'You've got to admit, Jamie, you wouldnae think it was worth anywhere near five hundred quid.'

'It's hard to tell, mate. I thought that helmet in the crates was a piece of shit. Could be that's worth even more.'

'We can find out. Melville's got books on antiques, so there's bound to be stuff like that in the library.'

The library was only a short distance away, on the Mosspark side of the lines. They skipped across, sneaked through the gardens and stopped off at the shops to treat themselves. Alex bought a stack of sweets from Missus Mancini in the cafe. Jamie bought only a bottle of cola, but it turned out that he'd nicked a handful of Kitkats, a silly move considering the money he was holding and that one of her sons was in the back shop.

'You cannae help yourself, can you?' Alex said, as they stood stuffing themselves outside the library on Arran Drive.

'I did help myself, ha, ha. Got to take your chances, mate.'

After downing the cola, they went inside.

Jamie spoke to the librarian who was on her knees stacking shelves. 'Any books on old stuff?'

'Old stuff?'

'Old stuff that's got something to do with China.'

'China the country or China Clay?'

'China the country.'

'Chinese antiques,' Alex said.

Squinting at them suspiciously, probably wondering why they weren't at school, she ran her finger over the book spines. 'Seven hundred to eight hundred is the art section. The seven forty-fives are your best bet,' she said and pointed to the ranks of shelves on the far side of the room.

At the section marked *700–800,* they pulled out books of all shapes and sizes and thumbed them from cover to cover, selecting the ones with pictures and stacking them on the varnished wooden floor. They sat and got to work.

Alex reached the bottom of his bundle and found nothing that resembled the Wee China. He looked around and noticed the thickest books he'd ever seen. He slid one from the bottom shelf, some sort of register of important people, set out in alphabetical order.

After skimming through the first few pages, he drew Jamie's attention. 'Hey, listen to what this says... Sir William Burrell, a millionaire shipping agent and a... a philan-thropist.'

'Sounds like a disease.'

'Seems everybody in here is called that.'

'It's someone who helps poorer people,' the librarian whispered.

Alex read on in a hushed voice... 'At the age of eighty-three, Sir William donated his famous collection to the people of Glasgow—'

'That's cause he got too old to do anything else with it,' Jamie said. 'He gave it away to feel less bad about himself after nicking it from the rice-eaters.'

'It says here it's priceless.'

'See? I told you, sure I did?'

'If this book is true, it means the stuff in the crates is ours by right.'

'How come?'

'Well, if Sir Willie gave it to the people of Glasgow, that's us. First come, first served.'

'Ha ha. That means we can flog it and keep the dosh and naebody can say nowt.'

'Right you are.'

The librarian, as they were about to go, ordered them to put the books back where they belong. She shook her head as they left a bundle on the top shelf.

'Don't want to put them in the wrong place,' Jamie said.

The talk on the way home was all about the get-rich raid they were planning on the mansion, with Jamie boasting about how easy it would be.

Shouting Distance

Saturday, Alex and Jamie hooked up with Forbes and McPeat, who were setting off to build a doocot. It was something to do at the weekends. Most boys built them for the fun of it and a place to hang-out, others took the sport deadly serious, competing against nearby doocots to attract homing pigeons out of the sky, catching them in netted frames to win the best, most expensive ones.

Although it was late October, it was cloudless and the sun was strong enough to heat the air. The rusting leaves and the greying grass were the only signs that winter was on its way, as the four of them sauntered along the paths in the Corkerhill allotments, where small gardens and sheds appeared out of nowhere like a lost village.

An old guy, waving his flat cap, called hello from one of the plots and came to meet them at the picket fence.

'Clock the conk,' McPeat whispered.

They couldn't miss it. The old guy's nose took up half his face, wide and long and pockmarked.

'What are you lot doing in these plots?' he asked.

'Nowt,' Forbes said. 'What're you doing?'

'I've come here every day since I retired. I like to keep watch on things. There's been a few vandals around here, you know.'

'Were you a polis mister?'

'I was a fireman stoker.'

'Did you put out any big fires?' McPeat asked.

'I didnae put them out, I kept them going… on the steam trains, shifting ten tons of coal on a single trip, Glasgow to London.'

'Ten tons, you sure?'

'That's how I grew this hooter... standing too close to the furnace,' the old guy said, taking the mickey out of himself.

The boys smiled at that.

'We're building a doocot,' McPeat said. 'Any old wood you don't need, any chance of a lend of a saw and some nails?'

'You can strip timber in yon boarded-up hooses, they're due for the chop any day now.'

'What about a saw?'

'I remember these railway hooses were the only hooses for miles. There'll be nothing left of them soon. Like old Nitshill, all that's left is a World War memorial and a—'

'What about a saw?' McPeat butted in.

The old guy went to his shed, moved tools aside, and took a rusty old saw from a hook on the wall. He passed it to McPeat, 'I hope everything doesnae look like it needs to be cut in half all of a sudden.'

Up on the hilltop, McPeat swiped it into an army of jaggy thistles, cutting them down and sending up puffs of white fluffy seeds that looked like tiny parachutes. 'Let's flatten them and build here.'

'Let's see who can kill the most with one swipe,' Forbes said. 'Here, give me a shot.'

Alex and Jamie left them to it and went to find timber for the base of the doocot. Reaching the fence of railway sleepers. Jamie squatted and used a stick to scratch out a map in the dirt of a dried-up puddle. He drew two crosses, pointed to them and talked like he was in a movie. 'That's Hardridge, and that's the mansion. We go straight over the golf course, over the garden wall… the windows have got prison bars so we jemmy the door, snatch the goods, high-tail it back here, bury it, and be back in our bunks an hour tops.' He lifted his head. 'I fancy that Jacob's pistol.'

'It's the Jacobites.'

'Aye. Them an all.'

'I'm going for that painting.'

'What planet are you on? We'll never shift a famous painting.'

A pair of foxes came out from the bushes, one after the other. They stopped and sniffed the air, both with a front paw raised, turned and looked at the boys, then trotted off.

'We could use one of them prams with the big wheels,' Alex said.

'Shift it doesnae mean move it, daftie. It means sell it. Anyhow, we'd be a right pair of morons trying to push a pram through the woods.'

'Suppose so.'

'What is it with you anyhow? D'you fancy that woman or something? You gonni put her on your wall like a Jane Fonda poster?'

'Shut it.'

'I must admit she's no bad looking. Might fancy her myself, ha ha.'

Alex stepped up to the fence and set about a fencing sleeper, shaking it back and forth until it slackened in the earth. It came away without too much fuss, just a squelchy sucking noise. They pulled out seven more and then went searching the bonfire scars for nails before heading back to the hilltop. When they got there, others had turned up — Grogan was sawing through a silver birch tree and Haw was chatting to Coggie and her pal from Mosspark, Rita Dougan.

Alex threw down the handful of bent and rusted nails that he'd picked up, some still attached to half-burnt chips of timber.

'Who gave the halfwit the saw?'

'Shut it. We're helping,' Grogan said. 'We've brought nails and a claw hammer.'

'Tell them to stick them up their arses,' Forbes said.

Everyone was looking to Alex, as if it was up to him to decide what happens next. He gave a shrug. That's how it worked — people who'd been fighting were expected to square things up, to 'sort it out' without holding a grudge, although he doubted that rule meant anything to headbangers like Grogan.

The two eejits helped to drag the oily sleepers up the hill and helped to tear corrugated tin sheeting from the windows of the railway houses. Once inside, Haw made a snide comment, asking Jamie if it was always so easy to break into houses, but Jamie didn't take the bait and no more was said about it.

The girls, in their good clothes, identical Fair Isle jumpers and jeans, looked on from the field as the boys ripped panelled doors from their hinges, chucked them over the balcony and carried them to the site, enough for a two-storey doocot.

Jamie knew how to build. He gave instructions for fixing the sleepers over the flattened thistles — two on their edges and the rest nailed on top like floorboards. With the base done, Grogan and Haw took over, nailing the doors to it, building up the sides and the roof and sawing off the overhangs.

Bored at standing around doing nothing, the others took turns of throwing McPeat's penknife at a target he'd carved in a tree. The girls got bored with that too and were about to leave when Alex talked them into going to the shop, giving them cash for sweets and juice.

They returned with a bottle of Solripe limeade and half a dozen packets of crisps. Coggie dished out the crisps and passed the limeade to Alex. The others pushed and shoved to get next in line behind him. He'd hardly taken a sip when Grogan snatched it from him.

'Hope you've no left your clatty floaters in here, Hannah,' he said, holding the bottle to the light.

'Give it back, fat-face.'

Grogan put his forehead against Alex's. 'Who you talking to?'

'Fight, fight, fight,' Haw chanted. He pushed Grogan's head from behind, smacking it into Alex.

Alex rocked on his heels. He stepped to the side, as if moving away, then brought his elbow round and up, putting all his weight behind it, full force. It caught Grogan under the chin, clapping his jaw shut and flooring him.

'Hit him again. You can beat him easy. Don't let him get up. Kick his balls.'

'Watch your big mouth, Forbes, you might regret it.'

'Shut it, Haw-Haw.'

Grogan got up and lifted the hammer. 'How about I use this?'

'How about we take that off you and knock your teeth in with it?' Jamie said.

'Pack it in!' Coggie screamed.

'Aye, c'mon get this finished,' McPeat said, climbing onto the doocot, trying to distract.

Grogan dropped the hammer and stood with clenched fists. 'I don't need that. I'll take you all on, one at a time. Square go.'

Rita held on to him. 'Stop it, Phil,' she pleaded, using his first name to soften him up.

'Hello the field!' came a croaky shout.

The old guy was standing in the long grass waving his cap. He pointed back to the path. 'Any of you know that woman? She's a wee bit confused.'

From the roof of the doocot, McPeat shouted, 'Alex! Forbes! It's your old dear.'

Alex sprinted through the grass and saw his mother. She was in her night coat, pushing Sarah in the pram towards the railway.

'Ma! Where are you going?' he said, blocking her way.

'I telt him to stay in shouting distance. He's wandered off.'

'Who?'

'Peter.'

Alex felt his insides folding, the dizzy sickness he got whenever something bad was happening.

'I'm in a hurry,' she said, trying to get past.

He held her arm. 'You better come home with us.'

She touched his bloodied eyebrow with her fingertip.

'What's the matter, Ma?' Forbes said, getting there.

'It's like a heavy black fog sticking to me.'

'C'mon home, Ma.'

'You okay, Missus Hannah?' Coggie asked.

'Did you take a wrong turn, Missus Hannah?' Haw said.

'Take a turn,' Grogan laughed.

Coggie gave him a two-palmed push in the chest and he fell onto the grass laughing louder.

In the street, Da came bombing up to them. He hugged her and led her up to the house. Alex and Forbes bumped the pram upstairs, taking care not to waken Sarah. They wheeled it to the living room and sat looking at everything except each other while Da talked to Ma in the bedroom. It was a long time before he appeared.

'I went to put a line on at the bookies,' he explained. 'I stayed for the race and by the time I got back she was gone. I've been hunting everywhere. I chapped doors. I mean, you'd have thought somebody would've seen her.'

'She's acting all weird, saying she's gonni find Peter. What's wrong with her?' Forbes said, twitching.

'Her mind is a wee bit mixed up right now. I'll call the doctor. Aye. I'll go and use Missus Little's phone and call the doctor. He'll fix things.'

Social Workers

The neighbours put on dour faces and sad voices. 'How's your mammy? Poor soul. Is she okay? Is there anything we can do?' She was fine, Alex told them. He thought they were only after gossip for the bingo hall and bus queue, but it was more than that because social workers came to the house. Someone had got on to them.

Da acted calm, inviting them in and offering them a seat on the couch, while he sat forward on the armchair waiting for them to speak.

The social worker woman, in a baggy black and white chequered coat, and a thick gold chain that dangled from her chubby neck, sat grinning nervously, with her rosy hamster cheeks and bright orange lipstick, some of it on her teeth. Next to her, the man kept taking off his specs and putting them on again.

'Is Missus Hannah at home?' the woman asked.

'In bed,' Da replied, his stare going nonstop from her to the man. 'Her medicine makes her drowsy.'

'We understand it must be hard for you, Mister Hannah. We're here to support you.'

'What's the fuss? There's nae need for social workers in this hoose.'

'We've had a call from someone expressing concern over your wife, and we—'

'Hold it a minute. Let's get this right, she's—'

Now the man interrupted. 'Mr Hannah, we also have a written report from last year. Your wife was found in a distressed state wandering around the derelict tenements in Abbotsford Place in the Gorbals. More recently we've received an account of her on the railway with the baby. It's not something we can ignore.'

'Where did you hear that shite? I'll go get her. Talk to her yourself.'

'We're only thinking of everyone's best interests,' the man replied. 'The safety and wellbeing of your wife and children are paramount. We don't think she's able on her own.'

'What d'you mean... able on her own?'

'We'd like a doctor to see her. She may be better off in Hawkhead for a while. Have you ever considered that?'

'The loony bin! That'll be fuckin right!' Da rose from the armchair, collared the man, dragged him down the hall and flung him out the front door.

The woman waddled behind. 'There's no need for hostility, Mister Hannah. We're only trying to help.'

'We'll be back with a court order. And you'll be charged with obstruction,' the man shouted from the landing.

Da marched out and kept pushing the man backwards until he was at the stairs. He grabbed the man's tie. 'Listen, smart arse, show your face here again and you're going over the balcony! You got that? You should've checked before coming here talking shite. She's already seeing a doctor.'

He cursed the nosey neighbours then noticed the boys' worried faces. 'It's fine, lads. They've been telt. They won't be back.'

That wasn't enough to settle Alex. The image of his mother in a mental hospital, doped and helpless, brought back the dizzy sickness. He wanted to run after the social workers and explain it properly. He'd heard the doctor talking about the new pills — one to be taken in the morning to lift her mood, one at night to help her sleep. That's what he'd heard. They didn't need to come back, she'd be fine.

When Da calmed down, he spoke slowly and intently, telling the boys to keep it in the family, to talk to no one about their mother, to watch their step now that the social workers had them in their sights. They could take kids away too. It had happened to families in the Gorbals, 'Boarding-out,' they called it.

Wednesday of the following week and Da was in his chair listening to a match on the radio. The signal was poor and the commentator's voice kept disappearing amongst crackling interference. It was time to mention the painting, Alex thought, sure that the idea of taking Ma to see it was a good one. If she saw the likeness, it might remind her of herself, like she was before. Imagine how she'd feel seeing it? It could help bring her back.

He plonked himself on the arm of the chair next to his father. 'What team you supporting?'

'Brazil.'

'Stop kidding, Da. Brazil's isnae even in it.'

'Brazil's isnae even in this country,' Forbes added. He was on the floor keeping Sarah amused with her building blocks.

'Shush lads, I'm trying to listen to the game here.'

'Do you want to know something?' Alex said.

'What's that?'

'There's a woman that's Ma's double.'

'Oh?'

'It's a painting in the mansion. We should—'

'A minute, son.'

Da slapped the radio, and the voice came back, loud and clear. '... *seconds remaining of the first forty-five. This free kick will be the last action before the whistle. It's on the nearside of the field in front of the main stand here at Hampden, just outside the eighteen-yard line... in it goes... the keeper's fumbled it...*'

A roar sounded on the radio and seconds later it sounded in the air outside like a giant sigh. Da jumped up and danced around, 'Gooaaal!'

Forbes got carried away too, and joined-in, hugging him.

'Up for the cup,' Da shouted.

Alex felt his blood rising at the sight of his father going bonkers over a daft football match when his mother was in a sorry state.

'Do you know what you're doing? Nothing. That's what!' he yelled. 'Do something to bring her back!'

'Calm yourself, Alex.'

'You don't listen. You're doing nothing to help.'

'Away to your room before I give you a skelp.'

His father had never hit him, never even threatened it.

Alex slammed the door on the way out.

Handers

It was too cold even for Homeless. The big mutt was curled up on the mattress that had been stuffed in the cellar for him. The sky was still half-dark and the streetlight was giving the frosted ground a tinge of orange. Shivering at the foot of the stairs, Alex was waiting for Coggie to leave for school. He waited ten minutes before deciding that she must have left earlier. Now he was late. He wouldn't rush, he'd only be sitting in class or walking the corridors bored out of his skull. Anyway, the 2E form teacher couldn't care less who showed up and who didn't, especially so near the Christmas break. Miss Cleghorn's science lessons were the only thing Alex liked about school. She took 2E for a double period once a week and often told him he was far too clever for that class. He stuck in at science and even finished the homework that she insisted on.

He didn't expect anyone to be hanging around at that time in the morning, but as he turned the corner he saw packs of boys on the hillside, their breath smoky white in the cold air — half the Toohill tribe, the Murrays, Wrights, Sinclairs, McGranes, Brodies, Curleys, Thomsons, McCanns and McLeans. Men too. Alex recognised them from the card school.

Forbes, Jamie and McPeat were together, the three of them blowing into their hands and hopping from foot to foot to keep warm. McPeat explained that Cammy Sinclair's cousin worked in a bonded warehouse in Kingston and had agreed to leave the fire escape open so that the men could walk right in and help themselves to crates of booze. They just needed help to carry it, and were offering a share of the takings.

Everyone staying off school, as if on strike, gave Alex a buzz. He felt as if he could steer clear of any trouble that came their way, but he was worried about Forbes.

'You better go in,' he told his brother.

'Who made you the boss?'

Alex was about to argue when Haw yelled, 'Ho! Clock the donkey jackets. What d'you call a bunch of Hannahs... a herd.'

It got a laugh.

Haw kept it going. 'Has your mammy sewed your name on it in case you lose it?'

'Pauper's gear,' Grogan piped up. 'Their old man cannae even afford a Provi cheque.'

'At least we've got an old man, your old man's a woman,' Alex blurted out. It was the only thing he could think of. But it was a good put-down, met with howling laughter, probably because Mister Grogan was a feared hard case, who regularly kicked the shit out of his sons.

Grogan smirked. 'Your ma's wired to the moon, Hannah, a fuckin spoon-licking spaz.'

There were only a few giggles this time.

Alex's blood rose.

'Pack it in,' Danny Toohill ordered.

Grogan turned and picked on the younger kids who'd started to wander off. 'Tell anybody about this and you're dead meat,' he shouted.

'Shut it ya fanny,' Forbes shouted back. 'You're already chopped liver.'

Alex grabbed Grogan's forearm and dug his nails in. 'You talk about my ma again and I'll fuckin batter you.'

'Anytime, Hannah,' Grogan said, yanking his arm away.

Alex, Jamie and McPeat were walking ahead of the mob in Corkerhill Place, when Nathan Coghlin came cycling towards them on a squeaky grocer's bike, a basket of food below the handlebars. He was in his army parka with the Ban the Bomb emblem.

'Alright?' he said.

'What are you doing on that thing?' Alex asked.

'Got to earn a living, man.'

'What about art school?'

As the mob gathered round, Nathan got set to pedal. 'I got kicked out,' he said.

'Look! It's Jesus on a bike,' Haw shouted, and straddled the front wheel. He picked out a packet of fig rolls. 'Who's this for?'

Hands began rummaging through the groceries.

'Put it back! It's all Mrs Little's provision,' Nathan said.

That comment brought on their slagging patter...

'Provisions! What's that fuckin meant to mean?'

'You talk some shite.'

'Swallowed a fuckin dictionary.'

'Who you fuckin kidding?'

'Smart arse.'

Jamie reached for a bag of flour, tossed it up in the air and shouted, 'Bombs away!'

As the mob stepped back from the explosion of white dust, he pushed the bike, helping Nathan's escape.

Nathan cycled off, swaying from side to side, trying to sort the groceries with one hand and steer with the other.

'He should've faced up to them,' Alex said to Jamie.

'He isnae a fighter, he's spaced-out half the time with the wacky baccy.'

The mob paraded on, up Corkerhill Terrace, past the doocot site that was now another bonfire scar, and onto the railway path. They followed it further than Alex had been before, under the Dumbreck road tunnel, where rust-stained icicles hung overhead like a trap of bloody spears in a jungle movie, ready to plunge down on you without warning.

On the far side of the tunnel, frost-heavy hawthorn branches narrowed the path and hemmed them into single file close to the track. They walked on quietly, watching and listening for the train on the bend. Those at the front heard it first, scurrying under the trees, those behind doing likewise.

Judging by the shouts of 'Ouch ya bastard', it seemed as if the thorns were attacking everyone, piercing skin and snagging clothes, as the train zoomed past. The freezing draft of it made their eyes water.

The colony had stretched out, about half a mile, by the time the first of them reached Kinning Park junction. In clear view now, the stores and factories stood out behind the pylons of the Wemyss Bay line.

After a powwow about getting frizzled if you touched the electric tracks, Danny Toohill ordered Grogan and Haw to cross and suss out the bonded warehouse.

They came back pissed off. 'It's got a twelve-foot brick wall, barbed wire, Alsatians and nae open door,' Haw said, staring at Cammy Sinclair. 'See when you see your cousin, tell him he's a bigger bum than ten arses.'

Grogan punched Cammy on the forearm. 'We'll just walk right in, eh?'

'You sure you were at the right place?' Cammy said, rubbing his arm.

Haw punched him on the other arm. 'Is that the place that's got a big sign saying *HRM Bonded Warehouse*, eh?'

Danny Toohill nodded to his cronies, and they headed up the line towards Central Station. Grogan, Haw and a few others cut into the streets at Pollokshields.

The rest of them went back down the railway path. At the Mosspark signal box they crossed the tracks, cut through the gardens and over the road to the shops. They took empty lemonade bottles from the crates in the lane, carried them round to the front of the cafe, bundled their way inside and claimed the refund, ordering boiled sweets from the jars on the shelves.

Missus Mancini, alone in the shop, shouted at them, 'One at a time, please.'

Each time she turned to lift the jars, they helped themselves to every chocolate bar in reach.

Alex, Jamie and McPeat were still in the lane. Jamie had cracked opened the back door. They could see Mrs Mancini at work, they could also see the cigarettes.

'One of you keep watch on the road, in case her sons show up,' Jamie said.

'It's too risky.'

Jamie stared at Alex as if he couldn't believe his ears. 'I keep telling you, mate, you've got to take your chances when they're slapping you in the face.'

McPeat flapped his arms and clucked like a chicken. 'Bwok, bwok, bwok.'

In the seconds it took Alex to walk to the road, Jamie and McPeat had piled up six cardboard boxes full of Embassy Regal, and in less than five minutes the three of them had crossed the tracks and were over the ash flats and in the woods, each carrying two boxes. They stuck to the forest path, up round the farm to the hillside at Corkerhill Road where they had met earlier that morning. They stashed the goods under the gorse bushes and went into the scheme to wait for the ice-cream van.

Jamie flagged it down on its first run of the evening. He made the deal, settling for half of the wholesale price, forty-five quid, which 'Two Scoops,' the ice-cream man, insisted was double the money he earned in a month.

'I bet those bampots think they're doing well with a couple of Mars Bars and a handful of gobstoppers,' Jamie said, dishing out the cash in an even three-way split.

McPeat tucked his share down his sock. 'Bet they wish they'd stuck with us. Never mind your Mars Bars, it's Black Magic deluxe for me.'

'I'm buying a denim jacket with this,' Alex said.

'Dead easy, mate, eh?'

Alex reminded Jamie of the 'dead easy' comment every time they heard a Mancini brothers' story. Angelo and Frank Mancini came hunting. Their souped-up Vauxhall Cortina was seen in Hardridge and it was seen outside the school gates. They pulled up kids, quizzing them on the knocked off smokes. They even slapped around one of the Toohill twins and locked Cammy Sinclair's head in their car window and threatened to drive away. The rumours got more and more far-fetched — they carried guns, they fired into the playground, they chopped off a boy's fingertip. Most were a load of rubbish, but one had Alex rattled — the one about them hunting for Two Scoops, the ice-cream man. He was off hiding when they went to his house, so they slapped around his old father instead. If it was true, apart from the nastiness of beating up an old man, it meant they knew where the cigarettes ended up, so it wouldn't be long before they found out about Alex and his pals.

Pond

Instead of school, Alex hovered around the workmen's fire with Jamie and McPeat, watching bulldozers destroy the railway village. Screeching steel jaws ripped iron palings from the balconies and stairways and chewed chunks of bricks from the outside walls bringing them down in a cloud of dust that rose into the cold clear sky, fogging over the winter sun and moon. As it settled, wallpaper patterns came into view on the still-standing walls, behind broken pipes and shattered timbers, like the bomb scenes on telly.

When the bulldozers attacked again, they brought down the roofs, the dust rising higher and falling further than before, peppering the frosted ground.

'Nothing much happening now,' Jamie said. 'Who fancies going to the pond? See if it's frozen.'

The pond was at least a mile away, in Pollok Park. Going to see if it was frozen wasn't the real reason for heading off — they knew it'd be safer in the park in case the Cortina appeared.

Out of the shop came Coggie and Rita, both with their schoolbags draped over the shoulders of their brown duffel coats, both wearing white woollen hats and white gloves and both chewing gum.

'You'd think it was cold or something,' Alex said.

Coggie smiled at him, the way she did, squinting her eyes, her whole-face smile. 'Well, the brass monkeys won't be very happy,' she said, knowing how to embarrass the boys.

'How come you're no in school?' Alex asked.

'Got sent home cause the pipes burst so you can stop hiding.'

'Naw we cannae,' McPeat said. 'The Mancinis are hunting us. And they've got guns.'

Jamie's hands were deep in his pockets. He used his shoulder to bump McPeat. 'Stop exaggerating. Naebody's hunting us.'

'Everybody knows you've got their ciggies,' Coggie said.

'I'd get the blame anyhow. I always get the blame. I'm no waiting around for the Mafia to show.'

'See when you think about it... the Mancinis are worse than the Mafia.'

'Give it a rest, McPeat.'

He closed one of his nostrils with his finger and blew a lump of snot out of the other.

Rita turned her back. 'I'm gonni be sick, ya dirty wee scunner.'

He wiped his nose on the sleeve of his jumper. 'It isnae my fault, is it? It's the cold. It's nipping my nose, so it is.'

'We're off to try the ice at the pond, want to go?' Alex said.

'Why not?' Rita replied and took his arm. 'Lead the way.'

Coggie took his other arm and giggled at his awkwardness.

They walked, the five of them, through the woods to the pond, their breath fogging up in a cloud over their heads as they stood along the edge staring at it. Shadows of trees stretched all the way across the grey frozen surface, dappled here and there by flashes of orange and yellow sunlight that made it through gaps in the branches.

Alex pulled at an overhanging branch of a willow tree that was stuck in the ice. It wouldn't budge. He tested his weight close to the bank, stomping a foot and then jumping. He walked out, and the others followed, checking their own weight then running and gliding with outstretched arms.

'Anyone for hockey?' Jamie said, swinging an invisible stick at an invisible puck.

They formed a daisy chain with McPeat at the speedy outside position. He let go, showing-off, crouching and spinning, and crashing into the bushes on the island. A pair of swans flapped their wings at him.

Rubbing his backside, he got up and pointed to a watery hole in the ice, small cracks at the edges. 'Hey! That looks like a spider,' he said.

Rita bent to study it. 'More like a reindeer with antlers and a—'

A pinging sound rang out across the ice.

It stopped.

It started again, like ringing glass, echoing and colliding.

The ice moved, creaked and groaned. Bubbles rushed along the underside.

Coggie and Jamie got on their tiptoes. They were nearest the bank. Rita and McPeat crawled on all fours.

Alex was furthest from safety. The island was only a few yards away on his left, but the swans were stretching their long snaking necks, hissing and flapping. He moved towards the bank, sliding his feet without lifting them.

'Looks like he's got cack in his pants.'

The fog from Alex's breath was coming fast. 'Shut your gob, McPeat,' he just about managed to say.

Everything sounded in slow motion as the ice folded up and over — a heaving crash of water, a fanning noise in the air and a fussy cackle coming from the bank. Slow sounds that sped up all at once. He was hearing the swish of the swans' massive wings, and the squawking laughter of his friends as he stood in the freezing water up past his knees, blood pulsing through his temples.

Coggie, doubled-up like she'd seen the funniest thing in the world, said, 'Better get out of there quick or you'll get stuck like that tree.'

He took a deep breath and used his heel to break the ice, clearing his way through the freezing water.

Coggie and Rita gave him a hand up to the bank.

'I cannae feel my toes,' he said.

'We need a fire,' McPeat said, rattling a box of matches. He lit one and let it fall. 'Boy Scouts.'

'They'd never let you in the Scouts,' Rita said.

As the kids began to move off, the swans eased into a long smooth glide, landed gawkily on the ice and waddled to the waterhole that Alex had made.

They set the fire at the base of the fallen sycamore, placing rocks in a circle and scooping in handfuls of kindling — frosted leaves and twigs that were mixed with frozen worms and slaters. McPeat dragged a match across the striking edge of the box, cupped his hand around it and held it to the leaves. The flames stuttered and died. He kept trying, using almost the whole box, two and three matches at a time before Rita took a jotter from her schoolbag, tore off the pages and rolled them into fire sticks.

'Girl Guides,' she said.

It did the trick. The fire popped and spat to life, and once the twigs got going, they added bigger ones, then branches.

As licks of yellow and blue flames cracked the cold air, Alex hung his socks and shoes on the jutting roots and sat with his back against the clay of the upturned earth. The others settled in beside him, each of them holding a stick to the fire, jiggling the burning branches and watching the popping embers rise towards the treetops.

'Jamie, what do you keep thieving for?' Coggie said out of the blue. 'It's bad and stupid.'

Alex shrugged when Jamie glanced at him, trying to make it clear that he hadn't told her anything.

Jamie reached for a fat branch and chucked it on the fire causing a flurry of red embers. 'It isnae bad if you're a master thief robbing diamonds from millionaires,' he said. 'And it isnae stupid. You've got to be dead smart, working everything out, having an escape plan in case you get disturbed and keeping dead quiet, cool and light-footed, like a ninja.'

'A ninja? Grog-on's got nae chance then. A baby elephant more like,' said McPeat.

'My daddy says people who steal from the rich get done big style. That's why them train robbers got twenty-five years,' Coggie said.

'For stealing a train?' Alex said.

'Don't be daft... for robbing money from a train. The queen's money.'

Alex nudged her arm with his elbow. 'Got you!'

She took off her woollen hat and pulled it down to his chin. 'Very funny.'

He lifted it and left it sitting high on his head. 'Tell them the joke about rich folk that Nathan telt us... the Highlander one.'

'This fire's making me sleepy. You tell it, you're better at it.'

'Let me think. I'll need to remember it.' He checked that his socks and shoes were drying, while going through the joke in his mind. 'Okay. I've got it now... this big Highlander is out walking the fields when he bumps into the landowner, Lord Percival-Smythe. Lord Percival goes, *Get off my land this minute.*'

'You sure his name was Percival?' McPeat interrupted.

'It doesnae matter what his name was. It was something snobby.'

'Shut up and let him tell it,' Rita said.

'Lord Percival says, *Get off my land this minute, you're trespassing!* And the Highlander says, *How come it's your land?* And Lord Percival says, *It was passed down by my great-great-great-grandfather.* The Highlander says, *How come he got it?* And Lord Percival says, *Because he jolly well fought for it.* So, the Highlander rolls up his sleeves... *Well come ahead then. I'll jolly well fight you for it.*'

The others laughed as Alex mimicked the Highlander, fists up.

He sat back against the warm clay, watching the faces of his friends glowing in the firelight. A perfect moment of calm.

'I could spend the whole night here,' he said.

McPeat spat through his teeth. It sizzled to a ball on the hot rocks and shot away. 'You wouldnae say that if you were out here on your lonesome. The owls, they'd make you feart for starters. Their hooting goes right through your bones like a mad ghost. Gives you the willies, so it does. And there's the tumulus. You wouldnae go anywhere near that at night, it's spooky as hell.'

'A whatulus?'

'A graveyard full of dead people from thousands of years ago.'

'Go pap peas at the moon,' Jamie said.

'It's true,' Coggie said. 'My daddy took me and Nathan when we were wee. It's them mounds in the woods on Pollok Golf Course. It's a Bronze Age burial ground. There's creepy carvings on the trees.'

They stared at each other with eyes wide open, fake fear on their faces.

Rita asked if anyone had more stories.

'I've got one. It's about rich folk too,' Jamie said. He was sitting with his hands clasped behind his head. 'Because my granny helped this Jewish guy when he was ill—'

'This one's alright the first few times you hear it,' Alex said.

Jamie got up and stood at the fire. 'I'll start again... because my granny helped this Jewish guy when he was ill, his people invited us to their big posh place in Pollokshields. You should've seen it. Up a long curving driveway with monkey puzzle trees. They asked her to take a seat in the middle of this big room and these women lit candles and shut the curtains and the place went all creepy and they waved their hands like this.'

Jamie moved his hands in circles at his face. He was good at telling stories. He stared blankly into space, like he was remembering being in the room. 'They started chanting in this weird-as-fuck language and they took—'

'What's the bad language for? It isnae big,' Coggie said.

'Aye, okay, give us a break. I'm only saying it sounded weird. Anyway, they took turns of holding my granny's hands. I was pure feart. I didnae know what to do with myself. Then someone opened the curtains, and it was over. I found out later that it was some sort of blessing. And guess what? We got the biggest feast ever. More fancy food than you could shake a stick at. Roast chickens, fish, dumplings on solid silver plates.'

He put on a posh voice, 'For afters we have a choice of pastries or bananas soaked in honey or fruit bread and for drinks we have chocolate milk or mango juice.'

'Did the monkeys get any?' McPeat asked.

'Eh?'

'The monkeys from the puzzle trees. Did they get any of the grub, the bananas and that?'

'Stop winding me up, McPeat. I'm no falling for it.'

'All this talk of food's making me hungry. We should go,' Rita said.

Coggie agreed, 'Aye, we better. The dark's getting here.'

McPeat ignored both and took his turn to stand and speak. 'I'm playing for Pollok under-fifteens on Saturday. The coach thinks I'm too wee, says I'll get pushed off the ball. He's letting me have a trial anyway, as a sub. Subs get to pick up dog shit before the game. It happened to Forbes. The coach gave him a stick to shift it but he wouldnae do it and there's no way I'm doing it neither.'

'Who's the best in the team?' Jamie asked.

'Dunno. We've got loads of good players. Forbes is a good goalie. He can nearly reach the crossbar without jumping.'

'Oh, that's all boys can talk about, football,' Rita said.

Coggie tugged at Alex. 'Let's go.'

'There's something up there,' Jamie said, pointing and putting a bit of panic to his voice.

'Aye, trees,' Rita said.

'Wolves! I can feel them staring, surrounding us, ready to pounce.' Jamie's voice was so convincing that for a split second it seemed like wolves were in the forest. Everyone shifted a bit in their places.

'Stop it. You're giving us the creeps,' Coggie said.

Jamie pointed again. 'What's that shadow? That's a wolf for sure. It's moving!'

Coggie moved closer to Alex. Her cheek touched his. 'Alex,' she said, gripping his arm.

McPeat took a burning stick from the fire and kicked it. Its flaming end glowed in circular trails of orange as it tumbled through the air. He lifted another, dropped it, held out his palms and looked up. The others turned their faces skyward and saw flickering shadows of snow falling above the firelight.

They waited for Alex to pull on his socks and shoes, and then scampered down the forest path. It gave way to a clearing where the railway houses had stood, lit by a blanket of snow a few inches deep and untouched apart from the tracks of an animal, most likely a fox out raiding the middens.

'It makes everything nice and clean and quiet, sure it does?' Coggie whispered.

The crump of their feet on the snow broke the hush as they walked on.

Home by six, Alex scoffed his food and was back on the street by half past, amongst the swarms of kids hurtling on upturned bin lids down the snow-packed hill, the snow falling again in big fluffy lumps.

The Cortina appeared later, after the younger kids had been shouted upstairs and older teenagers were hanging around on the corner. Its big exhaust pipe growled on the main road as it picked up speed, u-turned into the scheme and skidded to a halt.

Danny Toohill stopped Alex and Jamie from legging it.

'You don't run from these tubes,' he said. He booted the passenger door, trapping Angelo Mancini half out and half in.

At the same time, one of the twins bounced a bin lid off the windscreen, cracking it. The Cortina revved up as the boys gathered round it. It spat out black smoke and its wheels spun, going nowhere, churning the snow to slush.

The wheels stopped spinning. The car ticked over, rocking from side to side. A standoff moment.

Frank Mancini got out of the driver's side, hands at his head as if to surrender. 'Come on guys, there's nae need for this. We're only after our smokes, two hundred quid's worth.'

'Nae reason to come around here pulling up our boys,' Danny said.

'And spoiling our good snow,' Haw added, pointing to the slush below the tyres, and getting a laugh.

'We'll come back team-handed,' Angelo threatened from the passenger seat.

'Hope your shop's got insurance,' someone said.

'And your hoose.'

'Okay guys. Nae hassles,' Frank said.

Danny Toohill knocked on the side window, 'Hey, Angela.'

Angelo ignored him.

'Hey, Angela!'

This time Angelo wound the window down a few inches.

'Your ice cream's shite, by the way,' Danny said.

That got a bigger laugh.

The boys pushed the car free and gave it a few slaps and bangs as it drove off.

Alex welcomed the protection they had given him, like he belonged. But he was having serious doubts about nicking the cigarettes in the first place. That spur-of-the-moment dare had brought too much trouble, just like the Wee China. If he nicked anything in future it would need to well planned, secret, and worth the risk.

Flit

A visit to the doctor and a fresh supply of her get-up-and-go tablets and Ma was fine. Alex watched as she lifted Sarah to the highchair, tied a bib round her neck, gave her a dry rusk to chew and began working the wringer, turning it with one hand while feeding in the wet washing with the other. When he took the handle, she stepped aside and ran her fingers through his hair, saying it was growing wild and that she'd need to be getting the scissors out.

There was no way she was getting near his hair with scissors, but it was the kind of attention he craved from her. The kind he might get more often if Peter wasn't occupying her mind.

On Friday evening Da took her to the social club. It was a good idea, Alex thought, for it would show the neighbours that everything was okay. No need for social workers at the Hannahs.

Wrapped up against the winter wind in her coat and headscarf, she looked more than ever like the lady in the painting. Da was smart too, in his suit and overcoat, not old and shabby like he had been. His face was glossy from shaving and his hair was combed back with Brylcreem. Before leaving, he tossed a bunch of comics on the couch. He'd kept them hidden for the occasion, to keep the boys occupied. The money he left on the sideboard was to pay the milkman and the loose change to spend at the ice-cream van. No squabbling, he ordered, and Sarah was to be down by eight.

Sarah had found her feet lately and kept herself amused with her holding-on walking. She tottered round the furniture and played with her plastic blocks, building them up and knocking them down. She behaved herself and only protested at nappy-changing time. Alex took a fresh one from the fireguard, lifted her at arm's length and laid her flat. 'Let's get you sorted, smelly pants.' On hearing the milk float, he quickly undid the safety pins, removed the nappy carefully, used the clean side to wipe her down and then dangled it in front of Forbes before placing it into the steeping bucket in the toilet. He grabbed the milk money, ran downstairs and met the milkman on the first landing.

'This is for the Hannahs. Save you the climb.'

The milkman counted the cash and marked off the payment in this book.

'Are you taking on any milk boys?'

'I've seen you skulking around in the mornings. What's that all about, eh?' He was stooped over so much that Alex was looking at the top of his flat cap.

'I feed the dog, Homeless.'

'Lucky you've still got all your fingers.'

'He doesnae bite.'

'What age are you?'

'Fourteen.'

'Fourteen?'

'And a half. Nearly fifteen.'

'You don't look it. Talk to your parents. If it's okay with them, be at the bottom of the road, six o'clock sharp Monday morning. Two or three days a week to give the lads a break. See how you get on.'

'I'll be there.'

'Learn the ropes and I might let you go full time.'

Ma and Da were home by ten. Sarah was asleep in her cot, Forbes asleep on the couch and Alex sitting on the floor by the fire watching telly.

'You're doing a rare job here,' Ma said. 'We need to go out more often.' She checked on Sarah, came back and used her hanky to wipe away a smudge of chocolate from Forbes's lips. It woke him. She sat next to him and spoke about her night out. They had shared a table with the Coghlins, danced to the Ceilidh band and won a prize at the raffle — a bottle of table wine. She was tipsy-cheerful, but not too pleased with Alex's milk round news. 'It isnae natural for boys to be out at that time in the morning. You'll end up shuffling around like a half-shut knife, like the milkman,' she said.

Da plonked himself in the armchair. 'And it might interfere with schooling. You don't want that.'

'But you said... said I was to find a job. And what about Forbes? How come he's allowed to keep his paper round?'

'Top marks that boy. No worries there. You, on the other hand, need to work hard to get out of that class of dumplings.'

'But Da, I'm always up early so I may as well be getting paid for it.'

'Well... maybe. If it's just for a few days a week, it should be okay. You'll need to pay towards your keep, mind.'

'I could murder a cuppa,' Ma said. 'Who's gonni make their mammy a cuppa?'

Alex rose to go make the tea, walking to the door without straightening up. 'Look at me, Ma. I'm a half-shut knife.'

She giggled at that.

His enthusiasm over her good mood came crashing down when he heard her crying in bed later that night.

'I see him in the street,' she sobbed. 'I hear him all the time. I wake thinking he's tucked up with his brothers. I wait for him coming home from school. I wait and wait... I'd do anything to hold him again. Even for a minute.'

'I know,' Da said.

'I should've taken better care of him.'

'Stop thinking like that, darling. It was the slums. A dirty slum disease. He's worth every tear, but we cannae bring him back. You need to accept it, for your own sake.'

After a restless night, Alex stood in the bathroom doorway. 'We should flit,' he said.

His father, shaving at the sink, turned away from himself in the mirror. 'Flit where?'

'Anywhere.'

'You like it here, why move?'

'The social workers... we should go and live someplace they cannae find us... in case they come back bothering Ma.'

'Don't start, Alex.'

'I heard her last night.'

'Your mother's a lot better. Stop worrying and go find something useful to do.'

That was Da sweeping things under the carpet as usual. It did nothing to change the muddled reasoning that Alex was forming in his head — his mother needed help and he was the one who could do something about it.

Persuading Nathan

The boys never talked much on the milk, as if it was a rule. They just got on with the business of jumping on and off the milk float, running with as many bottles as they could carry, laying them at doors and picking up the empties. It was easy to keep up, so long as you minded the orders — Morrison bottom left, one pint, Armour one up, two pints, O'Rourke two up, two pints, Jamieson three up, two pints, and so on. The milkman kept a list in case anyone forgot.

They finished on the main road before eight and walked along the quiet street together, happy that their shift was over, although still not talking much. Alex took food to the dog, finished his chores and left in plenty of time for school. That was the deal he made with Da. But Ma didn't like it. She kept wanting him to pack it in, saying she could never relax while he was out of the house so early. He couldn't understand that because her night-time pills knocked her cold until late in the morning.

At school, he spent the first couple of periods dozing off, and made little effort for the rest of the day. It went on that way for weeks, so it seemed like a miracle when the form teacher handed him a glowing report card and told him to report to Mister Paton in 2A. Within minutes, he was sitting in a class with boys who wore school uniforms... well, some of them did. A brainy class. He couldn't wait to get home and tell his parents.

He found out that it was all Miss Cleghorn's doing, using her influence with the male teachers. If he worked hard, she said, he'd soon catch up.

She never missed a chance to give a pep talk. 'I want you all to think about your future,' she said during a physics lesson. 'What choices you make today can make a big difference to the rest of your life. What do you want for yourself? What do people expect of you — your teachers, your parents, your pals? How do they expect you to turn out? Will you leave school on a Friday and go straight to work on the Monday? What job will you have? Think about it and write a career choice on the front cover of your jotters.'

She waited for them to stop scribbling. 'Now score that out and write a better job.' She gave them another few minutes. 'Now write something even better. Don't be a slave to people's expectations of you. Surprise everyone by aiming high, something grand or unusual for this school, a doctor, a lawyer, an engineer. Aim for university. You are all capable. Remember that whatever you do.'

'We call that romancing, Miss.'

'Ambition is free. Everyone should have one. If your ambition doesn't work, step back and think up a new one. There are too many pupils in the school who're allowed to not care. You must care. None of you should let whatever is going on in your home life get in the way of your education. You don't have people pulling strings for you. You have to carve out your own future.'

The questions started.

'How much do lawyers get paid, Miss?'

'More than a footballer, Miss?'

'More than Mick Jagger, Miss?'

'A lion-tamer, Miss?'

'There's a joker in every class,' she said. 'What about an acclaimed classical musician? Did anyone think of something creative like that?'

'What about those people who paint faces on Halloween cakes, how much do they get paid, Miss?'

'A donkey-handler at Saltcoats, Miss?'

'Pay attention. What do you think of engineering?'

No hands went up.

'You might have heard stories of Americans boasting about their buildings being much bigger and grander than ours... their skyscrapers and bridges? Well, our engineers were building the magnificent Forth Rail Bridge while they were still playing at cowboys and Indians.'

The class giggled at that.

'The point is, we're still building bridges while they're putting men on the moon. We're being left behind in the technology race because there is a shortage of engineers in this country. That's a good example of a career opportunity. Isn't it?'

'Yes miss,' came the chorus of replies.

'Keeping to the subject of science, does anyone know how they deepened the Clyde hundreds of years ago when it was too shallow for boats, when you could walk across to Whiteinch if the tide was low? How did the engineers make the river deep and narrow?'

She asked for hands.

Boys put on puzzled faces like they were trying to solve it, rolling their eyes and pinching their noses.

'A tough problem in those days, you would think. Well, first they built a wall in the river to divert the tidal flow, speeding it up. They then planted rows of jetty posts along the riverbanks. An engineered solution that worked. Does anyone know how?'

Still no hands.

'Anyone? I've already given you a clue?'

'The tide,' Alex said after a long silence.

'The tide. Exactly! Well done.' She drew a sketch on the blackboard. 'The tide swirled round the posts as it ebbed and flowed, stirring the silt on the riverbed and dumping it at the sides, making the river deep and narrow. That's how the boats got upriver.'

'The banana boats,' someone said.

Everyone laughed.

'Most of your grandparents came up the Clyde on boats, so watch who you're making fun of.'

There were other lessons that held Alex's interest. He latched on to chemistry, biology and maths, trying to work things out ahead of the others, although he still lost concentration, mostly during English lessons. What was the point in all that Shakespeare patter? Who talks like that anyhow? It was a different language, boring. Shitespeare.

When his mind drifted, he went back to thinking of his mother, like she was before Peter died. It led to his persistent daydream about the painting in the mansion house and how best to get his hands on it. He imagined lots of ways of getting hold of it. He could take it in broad daylight, just walk out with it under his arm like the guy who stole the *Mona Lisa*. He thought about it when walking home from school, watching telly and in his bed at night. Then, after seeing a film about a trickster who conned people by selling them imitation masterpieces, he decided he needed a fake.

A stuffy English class on the first warm and sunny day of the year was enough for him to leave school at lunchtime, catch a bus to town and walk to the furniture warehouse in Ingram Street where Nathan worked.

Nathan was wrestling a rolled-up carpet through the doorway. He tilted it over his shoulder and walked unsteadily along the pavement, behind a woman. He turned round, puzzled, as Alex took the weight off the back end.

'Hey! What are you doing in toon?'

Alex shifted his footing to get a better grip. 'I saw you fighting this thing and thought you needed a hand. You got a body in here or something? It weighs a ton.'

'Inch-thick Persian. Sixty quid she forked out for it,' Nathan said. He stopped walking and Alex didn't, causing them both to stumble.

'You're up to something... what?'

Alex looked around and shook his head to add a bit of drama. 'Cannae talk here. It's too dangerous.'

'What are you on about, man?'

'I'll tell you once we get rid of the magic carpet.'

They followed the woman to a Wolseley parked on St Vincent Street. She slipped a tip to Nathan and then opened the back door to let them wedge the rug inside.

'Ten pence,' Nathan mumbled as she got into the driver seat.

'Eh? She pays sixty quid for that and gives you ten pence for lugging it a mile. What a tight arse.'

'Shush, Alex. These folk will get you the sack if you glance at them sideways.'

They walked to the City Chambers and sat on the steps facing George Square. Nathan took a tobacco pouch from his pocket, tapped out just the right amount onto a cigarette paper, rolled it and drew the sticky edge over his tongue. 'I like it here at lunchtime when it's sunny. Have you ever seen so many good-looking chicks? Where do you suppose they go at night time, eh?'

'Dunno. Back to their pens, ha ha.'

'So, what's this big secret?'

'I'm needing a favour.'

Nathan took a puff of the roll-up, waiting to hear.

'You ever see a painting so good that it makes you want to cry?'

'Sounds heavy... but I know the feeling.'

'Will you draw a painting for me?'

'You don't draw paintings, you paint them.'

'Well then, will you paint a painting?'

'For what?'

'I cannae tell you if you're not gonni agree.'

'I cannae agree if you're not gonni tell.'

'It's for a decoy. Remember you telt me about the *Mona Lisa* getting pinched?'

'What of it?'

'Well, I watched a movie about this cool guy who swaps masterpieces with fakes and nobody ever twigs, not for yonks. And by the time they do, they huvnae got a clue where it is, and he's clean away, with a yacht and a bungalow on a beach, somewhere with coconut trees and white sandy beaches and—'

'You gonni get to the point any time before my lunch break ends?'

'I'm gonni nick a painting from Pollok Mansion and I need a replica to put in its place.'

'Your head's away with the fairies, Alex. That's only in the movies, it doesnae happen in real life.'

'It's a woman.'

'What's a woman?'

'She's called the *Lady in a Fur Wrap*. The guy who painted her is called El Greco?'

'I thought he was the leader of the Govan Team?'

'He's been dead for hundreds of years.'

'The leader of the Govan team?'

'I'm trying to be serious here.'

'What'll you do with this El Greco?'

'This is gonni sound really weird... you know how my ma hasn't been keeping too good. Well, I keep thinking she's the woman in that painting. I mean before my brother died and that. It's on my mind all the time... oh, it's too hard to explain. Could be I just want to nick the fuckin thing.'

'Sorry Alex, I didnae know that about your brother.'

'It's okay. Look, they'll be too busy searching for the antiques to give the fake a second glance.'

'Antiques? You sure you're not getting a wee bit carried away?'

'It's gen-up. We've nicked one already, me and Jamie. We got ripped off at the pawnshop.'

'You two'll get chucked in jail, me too. Aiding and abetting it's called. And I'll be the culprit, the ringleader, leading youngsters astray and all that. They'd throw the book at me.'

'I'm only asking.'

'You serious about this?'

'Aye.'

'Alright. I'll go and see what you're so fussed about, but it all sounds like big talk.'

'Right now?'

Nathan took a last draw of the roll-up. He blew smoke rings and flicked the stub onto the road. 'It's too good a day to be stuck in that dump. I need a breather. It's only for a look, mind. I'm promising nowt.'

'Sure. Just a look.'

'Don't want to risk my carpet-carrying career, do I?'

Hearing in Colour

They were crossing the gravel courtyard at the mansion when it struck Alex that he could be spotted and nabbed for nicking the Wee China. He hunched his shoulders and kept his head bowed. A teacher was leading a line of primary schoolkids down the marble staircase, watched by the guard at the door.

Nathan spoke to him. 'Okay to walk round?'

He turned and eyed them. 'Naebody stopping you.'

Alex led the way to the library.

The lady in the painting was different from what he remembered. She looked shy, but as dazzling and proud as ever. He didn't trust himself not to steal it right there and then.

Nathan moved up close to it, his nose almost touching the canvas. 'Nowt special,' he said, and without warning he did exactly what Alex had been thinking — he reached over the mantelpiece and pushed the painting upwards, freeing it from its hook. 'If anyone comes in, act daft and say we're studying it for an art project.' He lowered it to the floor, face down. 'See these wooden wedges? They hold the canvas in place. They'll slip to the side. We can take it now if you want.'

Alex came to his senses. 'C'mon. Put it back.'

It took a few attempts to get it hooked on the wall and straightened. By now they were giggling.

'Her lips are sealed. She won't tell anybody,' Alex said.

'Their lips are always sealed. You don't ever see teeth on these old portraits.'

'Well, you can give the fake a big set of gnashers like mine.' Alex grinned and clapped his teeth like a chimp.

'Roughly twenty-five by twenty inches. That's the size of it. From the tip of my pinky to the tip of my thumb, three times, plus a bit.'

'Oh, right. Got it.'

They left and walked round the house and over the arched sandstone bridge to the riverbank where they sat with their backs to the sun.

A flash of blue and orange dived into the water, a bird with a long pointy beak, as long as its body. It pierced a tiny fish and carried it away. Below the surface, schools of sticklebacks darted around, water striders walked on top and mobs of midges swarmed above.

The pebble that Alex flicked scattered the tiny fish and shimmied slowly to the bottom. 'You're worse than Jamie,' he said. 'Taking it off the wall like that.'

'Bolder than bold boy?'

'Bonkers.'

'Listen to who's talking.'

'To be honest, I was thinking the same, taking it right there, but they'd have our descriptions. Can you imagine our photofits on telly? Unshaven hippy youth with long blonde hair and hair band. There isnae too many like you around here.'

'Baby-faced accomplice, hair like a brush.'

'It's why we need a fake. If they don't miss it, they won't be looking for it and they won't be looking for us.'

'If it's good enough, it'll buy you time. But I still think it's all big talk.'

'What are you painting right now?'

'Oh... I'm stuck on a portrait of the socialist leader John Mclean, trying to depict him leading a protest march. I'm struggling to convey the image.'

Nathan often used clever words like that — words that got him picked-on, people calling him a smart arse, a Nigel, a dictionary eater. He was different though — when boys his age were at the football or drinking in the pubs he was on 'Ban the Bomb' marches or selling the Morning Star newspaper on the street corners with his father, a trade union official.

'It's like you said, Alex, about getting an image stuck in your mind. I know exactly how that feels. I get freaked when I'm painting. I see tone and tints and shades in everything. And you'll never believe this... sometimes I even hear in colour. I keep touching up, going over it again and again, cannae tell when it's done and don't get to sleep for thinking of it. I've even ditched a few after months of work because I couldnae get them exactly the way I wanted.'

'Is that why you chucked art school?'

'Nah, I stopped going to the studios. I hated all that abstract shite. The head honcho, the professor, he gives me a talking-to. Art students are meant to tackle all forms of art. But some are kidding themselves. I mean, there's this famous artist who painted squares and circles and grids that are supposed to have hidden beauty and deep meaning, spiritual order and all that mince. I telt the head honcho that if he needed to explain it, it isnae art. And being an artist isnae about copying some other punter, it's about having your own style. Like El Greco, he had his own style.'

'I know.'

'My old dear rented a lock-up so I can work without stinking out the hoose. I like it in there. Peace and quiet, away from the art school and those privileged posers who wouldnae piss on you if you were on fire.'

Alex laughed. 'Wouldnae give you a nod in the desert.'

'They're from rugby-playing schools... what d'you expect?'

Alex flicked another pebble. 'D'you know that the people who own these big mansions, own nearly all the land in the country?' he said, remembering what Mister Mackenzie had told him. 'Seems they stole it in the old times when they crushed the clans. That isnae all... seems they captured the antiques from other countries.'

'So you wouldnae be stealing them, you'd be setting them free. Is that you're thinking?'

'Aye, that's it exactly... setting them free.'

'Liberating them.'

'The El Greco's good, sure it is? Worth liberating.'

'To be honest, Alex, I like the idea. A protest, like stealing the Stone of Destiny. Still, you've got to think what'll happen if we get caught.'

'But we're no gonni get caught.'

'But what if we do?'

'But we won't.'

'It's jail-bait. We'll get done for forgery.'

'Who was the guy in the film who said, *You're giving off negative waves*?'

'Suppose I just copy it and don't sign it, that isnae illegal. Right?'

'Right.'

'There's a wee problem though... it's donkey's years old. The oils were different in those days, the pigments and that, so I'll never be able to get it exact.'

'How come it needs to be exact?'

'It could be a tester for me, a conquest to get every drop of light spot-on... to capture more than just the mood of it. A good fake will fool the so-called art experts. It'll be years before the penny drops.'

'Brilliant!'

'Some of it's pretty grey and faded, and her skin and lips are a bit on the peely-wally side. I'll need to make it look that way, but I'll give her a wee subtle touch of extra colour. Maybe lipstick. Then we can argue that it was never meant to be a forgery.'

'Lipstick?'

'Wisen-up, Alex. They didnae have lipstick hundreds of years ago when it was painted. At least I don't think they did. It's modern.'

'Ha, that'll be a good one.'

'I'll make the oils from powders and dyes like the old masters did. But I'll need to find a print to work from and I'll need to go back and check the original from time to time and you'll need to get me an old canvas that I can scrape clean.'

'Where'll I get that?'

'Try the Barras. Art students go there a lot... I might be able to use the scrapings for layering. It'll take at least seven coats.'

Barras

Sounds of radios on different channels, a kiltie playing the bagpipes and traders shouting cheaper and cheaper prices of meat and towels and cutlery as people jostled for bargains before somebody else got them. Amazed at it all, Alex watched for a while before making his way through the crowd, passing a tiny caravan with a sign saying that the fortune-teller was inside and would tell you everything you needed to know, then a tailor's dummy dressed as a German paratrooper, outside a stall selling army uniforms, replica guns, war medals and the like.

Two traders at a junk stall, a tall scrawny man and a wee beer-bellied woman, were sharing jokes with passers-by. She had a thick scar on her chin, wore a cardigan that came down to her knees and a money pouch tied below her belly. Him in a black leather jacket and trousers, black shirt, white tie and hair greased-up like Elvis's. They were friendly, listening with serious faces, heads bowed, as Alex told them what he was after.

Elvis repeated it, 'You're after an old canvas painting that's two foot by two foot, or thereabouts, for your art project?'

Alex's cheeks flushed as the scar woman yelled it at the top of her voice, 'Listen up! We've got a special order here from a budding artist... an old canvas painting that's two foot, by two foot, or thereabouts.'

In a babble of shouts, the order was passed from stall to stall as traders went rummaging amongst junk furniture from what seemed like hundreds of house clearances. They fished out paintings of all shapes and sizes and stacked them on the pavement for Alex to sift through. He was causing a fuss and wanted to pick one quickly and escape, but most were torn and threadbare, or not the correct height or width. He was holding one that was too big, thinking it could be cut to size, when a woman in a headscarf laid down a landscape of hills and sheep, framed in a carved wooden surround. She used a cloth measuring tape to show that it was the right size. It was covered in grease, and the paint was cracked and flaking but the canvas was intact.

'Could be okay,' he said.

'Maybes you're no letting on here, no telling us the score. Maybes this frame's worth a wee fortune,' said the headscarf woman, winking at the scar woman.

'You can keep the frame, it's just the canvas.'

'Two quid and it's yours.'

'Two quid? You're taking liberties there, Peggy,' the scar woman said.

Alex got ready to haggle. 'I've only got forty pence.'

The headscarf woman folded her arms.

'Honest.'

'New money?'

'Aye,'

'Okay, it's a deal, if you throw in a big wet kiss for me.'

'Stop embarrassing the lad, Peggy.'

Nathan answered the door, his eyes going straight to the canvas. He took it and carried it to his room, frowning as he studied it. He sat with it on his knee. 'Not too bad. Fine weave. Not bad at all. I'll clean it with acetone and restretch it'

While he was getting to work with a pair of pliers, Alex peeked inside Coggie's room. It wasn't tidy like he expected it to be. It was a jumble of scattered clothes and bed covers. A troop of dolls were bundled the windowsill and picture scraps were stuck to the mirror of her dressing table. With a sudden sense of trespassing he turned back to Nathan.

'How long will it take?'

'Six months to a year.'

'You're kidding. It's only supposed to be a copy, no a freaking Van Gok.'

'Van Gogh.'

'Him too.'

'I'm keen to give it a right good go in the traditional way. Broad brush on the background and seven layers of light touches of thinned-down colours on the face. I'll dry the last coat in front of the fire to make it crack, fill the cracks with dust, then wash in a mix of nicotine and varnish. It's an old faker's trick I read about.'

Six months to a year was far too long for Alex. Best to let Nathan get it started and then pester him to finish it quicker.

Howf

Jamie's granny was slicing peeled spuds in the palm of her hand and tossing them into a pot when she saw Alex in the hall.

'My, you've taken a fine fair stretch, Alex. Come in and sit at the table and let's have a good look at you,' she said in her soft Highland twang.

'He's here for a loan of my Levi's. We're off to the school disco the night,' Jamie said.

'Borrow, not loan.'

With her thick white hair brushed back tight from her forehead, bushy black eyebrows, leathery tan skin and big horsey teeth, she reminded Alex of the old Indian chiefs from the cowboy films.

She set down a plate of scones, took a jug of juice from the fridge and filled two glasses. 'Get stuck in.'

'My da's talking about getting a fridge,' Alex said, just for something to say.

She smiled at him. 'It's pretty handy... stops the milk freezing up in the winter.'

Jamie cut a scone in half and used a tablespoon to plaster it with jam. She clouted him with the wet dishcloth and moved the plate to Alex's side of the table.

'How's your ma?' she asked.

'Good.'

'Your da?'

'Good.'

'Are you helping out around the house?'

'I'm on the milk.'

She kept glancing at Jamie, like she was working up to something. She got to it moments later. 'Where are you getting the money for this disco?'

'The tickets are free... sure they are, Alex? Free tickets for nothing,' Jamie said, grinning.

'If you've been up to no good, you'll find yourself in borstal with nowt bar bread and water for your dinner.'

'What? Nae jam?'

'Aye, nae jam. And the back of my hand if I get any more lip.'

'Ask Alex. He got the tickets.'

'That's right, Missus Bryce. They're free. It's the end of term disco.'

'He needs to find a job to keep him out of bother. How about you putting in a word with the milkman?'

'Too early in the morning for me, granny. I'm gonni be a joiner.'

'So long as you don't get taken in by these adverts on telly, luring boys to join the forces. It's a bloody disgrace, so it is.'

'Watch out, Alex, she's getting on her soapbox.'

'I'm serious. They'll tempt you with their fancy talk and before you know it, you're on the front line getting slaughtered with all the other weans. Whole villages of boys wiped out in the First World War, shelled and gassed, my own two brothers alongside them. Weans they were, seventeen and eighteen, only a few years older than you two. All for the sake of a royal family argument. The Earl of Haig and his kind have a lot to answer for. They can stick their poppies.'

'I thought poppies were meant to stand for peace,' Jamie said.

'Ask any mother whose son didnae come back. They wouldn't need to sell them if they didnae keep sending weans to be slaughtered or injured. Just look at what's happening in Vietnam, all those—'

Jamie stood. 'I'll go get the denims so you can escape the ear bashing, mate.'

His granny threw the dishcloth at him. 'Washed and ironed and in your drawer.'

They met at seven, Alex in Jamie's cast-off jeans and a black T-shirt, Jamie in new Wranglers and an Arthur Black shirt with pleats at the back, a button-down collar and tartan flaps on the pockets.

'Been splashing out?'

'Nae point in hoarding it, like you. Try spending some of your dosh on a comb.'

Alex spat on his hands and patted his hair.

'Fancy downing a few beers?' Jamie said.

'How'll we get them?'

'Has your old buddy no been thinking ahead, mate? Of course I have. I've already got a stash. I'll show you... but only if you swear you won't tell anybody about my howf.'

'Your what?'

'My howf. A den. Do you swear?'

'I swear.'

'Promise to God?'

'Promise to God.'

'Right hand up?'

'Right hand up.'

'Swear you won't even tell Forbes?'

'Fuck sake!'

'Okay. I trust you. Follow me.'

They fence-hopped the palings in the back gardens to the spare ground behind the gable-end walls on Hardridge Avenue. Jamie got down on his knees and squeezed through a gap in the overgrown jungle of hedging and bushes. After crawling along a tight furrow with Alex at his heels, he stopped and pushed upwards on a hatch. Only now could Alex see the outline shape of the den, camouflaged in green tarpaulin and tangled ivy.

They hauled themselves inside.

'Mind your napper,' Jamie said, flicking a switch wired to a car battery. The place lit up.

'All the latest gadgets in here, mate. It's my hidey hole,' Jamie said, looking pleased with himself.

The howf was decked out with a folding camp bed, a Primus stove, a leather car seat, and a steering wheel screwed to the wall. Next to the camp bed was a wooden box. Jamie opened it, took out two bottles of beer and prised off their lids with his belt buckle.

Alex, in the car seat, held the steering wheel. 'What's this for? You playing at racing-drivers?'

'I got it from a sports car at the scrappy, an MG Midget. I'm only messing around with it,' Jamie said, passing over a bottle. 'I think it's worth a couple of quid.'

Alex took a sip of the beer and winced at the gassy, bitter taste.

'Six percent,' Jamie said. 'Foreign gear.'

'From where?'

'A cellar.'

'Whose cellar?'

'Don't know. Whoever it is, they've been thieving from the docks for years. You cannae get done for knocking something that's already knocked off, can you?'

'You'll get done if the docker catches you. Done in.'

'I only took a few. He'll never notice,' Jamie said, and swigged on the bottle. 'You don't get beer like this in the pub, eh?'

'Nah. You don't.'

'Ever been in a pub?'

'Nah. You?'

'Nah.'

Jamie stretched to the wall and slid back a piece of plywood, uncovering an opening that peeked through the bushes to the avenue. 'There's someone else with a hideout. See that broken-down car over there, the Hillman Imp? McPeat kips in there sometimes. I hear him going in at night when his old dear's boyfriend chucks him out.'

'What about his da?'

'He hasn't got a da, he just talks as if he has.'

'Why don't you let him kip in here?'

'Cannae. He's bound to slip up and tell somebody, and then everybody'll know.'

The howf felt invisible. No one in the avenue would have a clue that people were hiding only a few yards away. It was a perfect hideout.

Jamie explained that it had taken months to build. He'd cut the furrow using wire cutters, pulled timber planks along it, set up the base so it was off the ground, held it all together with woodscrews and covered it in layers of green tarpaulin — everything nicked from the college construction site.

Rifling the contents of the wooden box, Alex saw there were four more bottles of beer, a half-full bottle of Irn-Bru, packets of crisps, comics, a small two-pronged jemmy, gloves, loose change and an assortment of keys and wristwatches.

Jamie picked out one of the watches. 'Here, keep it. It's got a luminous dial. Pretty handy in the dark… If anyone asks, say you bought it at a jumble sale.'

'Where did you nick it?' Alex asked, fastening the leather strap to his wrist.

'At a jumble sale, ha ha.'

'What are the keys for?'

'Some's for cars, some's for mortise locks. The T shaped one opens all the cellars in the street and the piece of plastic slips the latch locks.'

'You ever worry that you're gonni get nicked?'

'I'm no planning getting nicked. I couldnae handle being locked away when everybody else is running around enjoying themselves.'

'I know,' Alex said.

'Naw, you don't. You've never been locked-up.'

'And you have?'

'In Dr Guthrie's. A home for kids. My ma done a runner when I was wee. Tossed her things in a suitcase and pissed off to London with her fancy man and left me with my alky Da, and he goes and gets poisoned cleaning a tank. Him and two other men. Stone dead, all three of them. They had to put me in a home, so it was Dr Guthrie's, just because I'd been caught stealing. My granny fought them in court, helped by her church pals. She got legal custody. It's been me and her ever since.'

'What did you steal?'

'A packet of biscuits... from the Co-op.'

'What kind?'

'Wagon Wheels.'

'Wagon Wheels?'

'Aye, I know. It's an embarrassment.'

They slugged their beers at the same time. The second one going down easier than the first.

Alex thought he'd try a tiny confession to even things up with the Wagon Wheels story. 'I drank all the syrup from a tin of pears once. Pierced a hole, just for a sip, only I kept going till I'd drank the lot. Come Sunday dinner, the pears had gone mouldy... they'd grown beards. My brother got blamed. Must've looked guilty.'

'Forbes?'

'Nah, Peter.'

'Oh... Crime of the century, mate. Did you own up?'

'Course I didnae.'

'You're worth the watching. Sleekit as your granny's cat, so you are.'

'I huvnae got a granny with a cat. I huvnae even got a granny.'

They spluttered their beer, giggling, drank more and then fell quiet for a moment.

'Jamie,'

'That's me.'

'I've something to ask you.'

'Ask away.'

'Who is it that's breaking into the hooses?'

'It isnae me if that's what you're thinking.'

'I'm not saying that.'

'I swear on my granny's life, mate, I've never done a hoose. Never. Anybody that breaks into people's hooses is gonni get lynched. Am I right?'

'Okay, I believe you.'

'Honest to God. I've done the railway station and the post office, never a hoose. I swear. It's some other bastard doing that. It isnae me. If my granny hears I'm being blamed, she'll send me to live with her sister in Inverness. She keeps saying it'll be better for me up there.'

'I didnae blame you. I only asked cause I heard rumours.'

'Here! Wait a minute. Listen to the pear-juice stealer who wants to rob the big mansion hoose.'

'That's different.'

'How?'

'It's a museum.'

'But people still live in it.'

'You sure?'

'Maybe.'

'Guess what? I've been back.'

'What for? Did anyone spot you? That wierdo Mackenzie?'

'Nah. Naebody even bothered us. I took Nathan to see the painting. He's gonni paint a replica, a fake that we can swap for the original.'

'What did you go and tell him for? He's a dopeheid. Couldnae put emulsion on a wall.'

'Nah. His stuff's amazing. He's sound.'

'I don't get it... it's the antiques, nowt else.'

'You keep on about it, Jamie, but are you ever gonni do it?'

'How about me going for the stuff in the crates and you going for the painting? I get a million quid and you get a poster for the wall.'

'Aye, that'll be right. I'm in for the antiques as well.'

'Now you're talking,' Jamie said, chinking Alex's beer bottle with his.

Coggie

Mister Paton, Alex's form teacher, blocked the way to the school disco, studying their faces at the door. 'Have you two been bevvying?'

'We're too young to bevvy, sir.'

'What? Have you always got that glaiket look on your face?'

He stepped aside, guffawing at his own joke. 'You'll be disappointed if you're hoping to pick up a chick... because you couldnae get one in a pet shop,' he said, laughing again.

In the assembly hall, massive speakers were blasting out T'Rex's *Get it On*. The girls were dancing below swarming disco lights and the boys were hanging around the sides trying to look cool. Not Jamie. On hearing the intro of The Faces' *Stay With Me,* he dragged Alex to the dance floor and tapped the nearest two girls. Even with the glow of alcohol Alex felt stilted, his arms and legs just wouldn't connect with the beat, a nothing-like-dancing dance, especially next to Jamie who was drawing attention with his Rod Stewart moves, marching in close to the girls, making them giggle, marching back out again. At the next record, *Jumpin' Jack Flash,* he tugged on Alex's sleeve and nodded towards the best-looking girl in the world. 'Who's she?'

'That's Lorna Edwards.'

Alex fancied her like mad, and so did every other boy in the school. She stood out with her brown skin, dark eyes and perfect smile, and looked more like a grown woman than a third-year girl.

'You've nae chance with her.'

'We'll see,' Jamie said, and with everyone watching, he walked up to her and tapped her for a dance.

She gave him a dirty look, turned her back and carried on dancing with her lanky pal.

Ignoring the knock-back, he tapped her again. This time, he rubbed his eyes pretending to cry and then quickly moved on to the next pair of girls.

Dancing, record after record, wasn't so bad after other boys found the courage to get up. Still, Alex was glad when the DJ played a track from a Led Zeppelin album that nobody knew, and the floor cleared in seconds. He and Jamie joined the queue for drinks, waiting for Miss Cleghorn to finish pouring syrupy cola into rows of plastic cups.

'Need a hand with your cups there, Miss?' Mister Paton said, ducking under the hatch to get behind the counter. He winked at the boys.

'He's a creep,' said Lorna Edwards, standing behind in the queue.

'Help me out here, mate. Talk to her pal.'

'No way. Her nickname's Wingnut.'

'C'mon mate. I'd do it for you, talk to her for a minute.'

'Nup.'

Jamie gestured to let the two girls through to the bar.

While Wingnut was ordering the drinks, Lorna faced up to him. 'D'you think you're Mister Big or something?'

He placed his hand at her elbow. 'Listen, Lorna, can you do us a favour?'

She gave a suspicious stare.

'My mate fancies your pal. Will you ask her to come and meet him?'

'Shut it,' Alex said.

'She already knows Alex Hannah,' Lorna said.

'Well that's even better cause he's shy.'

'You're not at this school, are you?'

'I'm at uni.'

'What are you studying?'

'Eh... law.'

'Doubt it,' she said, then whispered something to her pal, and seconds later Jamie was leading her to the dance floor.

The set up was too quick to avoid. Alex was left with the giggling Wingnut. She was taller than him, skinny as a rake, and her ears stuck out. He thought about making an excuse and walking off, but that would embarrass her.

She stood holding the drinks and offered him some, grinning shyly.

He shook his head.

She nodded towards the dancers. 'D'you want to?'

'Nah. This music's crap.'

'C'mon, everybody loves *Wig-Wam Bam*, everybody's dancing,' she said, and laid the drinks on a table.

She was tugging at him when the disco lights changed to ultraviolet, making her teeth, dandruff and bra glow in the dark. She crossed her arms over her chest and ran for cover.

Alex slinked off to blend in with a group of boys hanging around the DJ. He spied Coggie. The freckles on her face and arms stood out in the ultraviolet light. She seemed older in her summer dress and heels. Rita was also drawing attention and when the slow music started, two fourth-year boys tried to move in. Both girls stepped to the side and made for the exit.

He caught up with them at the cloakroom. 'I didnae see you two in there,' he fibbed.

'Hiding from you,' Rita said, collecting her leather jacket. 'Saw you with your new girlfriend. Where is she?'

'She's chucked me.'

'Poor boy, it wouldnae have lasted anyway,' Coggie said. 'You'd need ladders to whisper sweet nothings to her.'

'With them ears? I don't think so.'

They passed Mister Paton at the door. 'Hey, Hannah. How can a pair of uglies like you and your pal pull two chicks each? These lassies must be feeling sorry for you.'

'You're jealous, sir,' Rita said.

Alex and Coggie saw Rita to her house in Mosspark, then made their way up past the railway station to the main road.

'Forbes and McPeat are playing in a big match the morra,' Alex said. 'A play-off for the league. Everybody'll be there. D'you fancy it?'

'Don't think I can. I'm going to see about a job in the Ceylon Tea Centre. It's Shawlands afterwards, with Rita. We're meeting girls from school for a coffee.'

'A coffee. That's posh.'

She leaned against him. 'I see Casanova's hit it off.'

'Eh?'

'Jamie. He's walking Lorna home.'

'Girls fancy him somehow. I don't get it. Paton was right, he's got a face like Plug.'

'It's you they fancy, Alex. I hear them in the playground talking. They're always on about you.'

Her comment caught him flat. He had walked her home from school dozens of times, yet he suddenly felt awkward and wished he had Jamie's confidence.

'What's up, cat got your tongue?' she said, her ice-blue eyes narrowing as she smiled. 'Or is it because Jamie got off with Lorna and you didnae?'

'I'm doing alright,' he said, thinking it sounded quite a good thing to say.

'Oh! You don't think... me and you, do you?'

'I'm fussy you know.'

'You could do worse,' she said, stopping to undo her shoes and holding on to him for balance. 'These heels are killing me.'

She walked on, bare footed.

'Better watch out for dog shit.'

'Give us a shouldery then.'

Alex squatted on his heels. 'Climb aboard.'

She tucked-in her dress and swung her legs across his shoulders, and he hooked his arm around her shins and lifted her off the ground.

'Fares please,' he said, holding out a hand.

She leaned down and made a face, pulling on her ears and crossing her eyes.

He pretended to lose balance. 'Shouldnae clown around distracting the driver, you might cause a crash.'

Rain began to fall, drizzle at first, but it was soon drumming on the parked cars. They had no jackets, but it did not hurry them. She made her wet hair fall over his face, blocking his view. This time she held his cheeks and gave him an upside-down kiss on the lips.

The moment ended in an angry shout. 'Shona Coghlin! What are you playing at? Get up here right now!' Her father was at the living room window.

Alex set her on the pavement and she ran upstairs, her wet dress clinging to her skin. 'Bye bye,' she said and waved without turning.

Sweet

Nethercraigs sports ground, a short walk down the hill, was made up of red-ash football pitches and a showpiece grass one facing the pavilion. The league-decider was played on the grass pitch because of all the interest in it. Scouts from Celtic, Rangers and Partick Thistle were supposed to be there looking for good players. But the game was scrappy, the ball skidding off the rain-soaked ground, bouncing off players or flying under their feet as they swiped at it. They were having a hard time trying to stay upright on the churned-up surface. Even the ref was mud-splattered from head to feet.

Alex kept checking the sidelines for Coggie, but she didn't show.

Da would not leave Ma on her own for too long, so he didn't arrive until after the second half got underway, in time to see the ball glancing off Forbes's gloves into the net for the opening goal.

When Harmony Row's celebrations died down, their coach shouted, 'Shoot from anywhere. They've got a skelly-eyed keeper.'

Forbes was raging over it, twitching as if trying to shake something from his shoulders.

'Don't react to that baldy wee nob. Keep your discipline,' shouted the Pollok coach.

At 1-0, the Harmony Row players were doing their best to waste time, taking ages over throw-ins and free kicks, faking injury, fouling and booting the ball in the river whenever they could.

The Pollok supporters hassled the ref at every turn, howling at every decision that went against their team.

'Better be adding time on ya blind poofter.'

'See that big number five... he works nightshift doon the mines. This is meant to be under-fifteens.'

'Cheating bastard, you're on the take.'

McPeat, the smallest and skinniest player on the park, the only one to stop and put his foot on the ball, kept catching defenders off balance. They slid past, giving him space. He was on the ball more than anyone. He didn't wait for it, he ran to meet it, turned to follow it, speeding up and slowing down, changing direction left and right. He was running in on goal when a two-footed, studs-up lunge wiped him out.

'Good challenge,' shouted the Harmony Row coach as McPeat lay in the mud wriggling and crying.

Alex turned at the sound of Da's voice. 'Forbes!'

Forbes was charging towards the Harmony Row sidelines. 'I'll show you a good fuckin challenge!' he yelled and flew into a long sliding tackle that took the legs out from under the baldy coach and sent him up in the air.

After the melee, pushing and pulling and a few swinging punches, the ref sent off Forbes.

Pollok scored from the free kick to equalise and while the players were rolling about hugging and kissing, the ref allowed Harmony Row to restart. They walked the ball into the empty net and he blew for full time straight away, already sprinting to his car. The goal that he gifted didn't even embarrass the Harmony Row lot. Their players celebrated like crazy, rubbing it in.

As the Pollok coach and a mob of supporters went after the ref, fighting started on the pitch. Da had to stop Forbes from getting in the mix, pulling him away.

At least it was something to talk to Coggie about. Alex had been building up courage to ask her on a date and wouldn't want to run out of things to say on the night.

When he called at her house later that afternoon, she came to the door, took his hand and pulled him inside to listen to a record that she had bought in Shawlands, *The Locomotion*. Her room had been done up, all neat and tidy. He sat on the bed and she danced around singing along to Little Eva, using a hairbrush as a microphone. She was happy, she said. She'd been offered a Saturday job and was due to start work the following week.

It was now or never. At worse, she'd make a joke over it. 'D'you fancy going to see a film with me?' he asked.

She stopped and sat next to him, her bare arm touching his. He thought of the kiss and got goosebumps again.

'Of course I do. What about *The Godfather*?' she said. 'I'd love to see that. They've been talking about it on telly.'

There had been loads of hype about it, but Alex knew all the films showing in town and it wasn't one of them.

'I'll keep a watch out for it,' he said. 'It'll be coming to the ABC or the Odeon.'

'It's an eighteen. Will they let us in?'

'We can give a false date of birth if they ask.'

Just then, Nathan and Mister Coghlin arrived home from their stint of selling the Morning Star in town. Mister Coghlin opened the door and gawped at Alex. 'She'll be getting her dinner soon.'

Time for him to leave.

Nathan was in the hall holding the scraped-clean canvas. 'I'd say this is pretty near perfect. No telling how old. A hundred years at least.'

'Perfect for what?' Coggie asked.

'He's doing a painting for me. A pressie for my ma.'

'Oh, sweet boy,' she said.

Monty Walks

It couldn't have gone better, Coggie had snuggled up to him all the way through the film and now she held his arm as they strolled down Renfield Street amongst the Friday night revellers in town.

Outside MacSorley's pub, she cracked open the door with her foot. They dared each other to go inside, and then stumbled into a line of men at the bar who straightened all at once, turning to stare. They ran out laughing. They laughed again at the funny chants of the man selling the newspapers on the corner, and at the drunk who walked the bus queue blowing a harmonica while holding out his hand for pennies, and they couldn't stop themselves when an old woman told him to piss off, laughing so much that they didn't notice Hardridge boys jumping from the number 50 bus.

Dressed in their double-breasted suits and bright wide-collared shirts, they gathered round the couple, each of them with a bit of patter...

'Have you lost your mammy and daddy?'

'What are youse two doing out in the dark?'

'That's no fair. They're all grown up.'

'It's Mister and Missus.'

'Who's watching the weans?'

They ruffled Alex's hair, messing him about, but it was a friendly reception. He'd been spotted out on a date with Coggie, which would bring no end of admiration. And she was leaning on him beautifully, her arm around his waist. Girlfriend and boyfriend.

'Where have you been, doll?' Haw said.

Her long blonde hair had fallen over her face. She raised her arm to brush it aside. '*The Godfather*.'

'An eighteen. Cool,' he replied, nodding as if impressed. 'Fancy a night on town with the big boys? Alex can find his own way home.'

Her cheeks flushed. 'All I see is a bunch of drunken neds.'

'My buddies are very respectable I'll have you know.'

Cammy Sinclair lifted a traffic cone and stuck it on his head. 'Respectable? Of course we are!' He did a funny Monty Python walk along the middle of the road and four more of them fell into line, copying him.

As Coggie went to step onto the bus, Haw held her arm and placed the flat of his hand against back. She brushed him off.

'The film was amazing, sure it was?' Alex said as the bus crossed Jamaica Street Bridge to the Southside.

'Best ever. I loved it. Al Pacino was great in it. I cannae wait to tell Rita. And that bit with the horse's head, yuk!'

They had been chatting well all evening, no awkward silences, and Alex didn't have to rely on his saved-up stories. 'What's it like in the Tea Centre, any good?' he asked.

'You meet lots of people. I like meeting people. I might get a hairdressing job when I leave school.'

'You might get nits,' Alex said, with a half-smile.

'It's good pay in the top salons. Not at first, but after you get qualified and that. What about you, what will you do when you leave school?'

'Haven't thought that far. Miss Cleghorn says if I stay on, I can go to uni.'

'Ha, you're her wee pet.'

'It's as bad as school,' she said. 'And remember what happened to Nathan? He got booted out cause he didnae fit-in.'

Alex was trying to impress. He wouldn't have mentioned university if any of the boys were around. Feeling as if he'd said something daft, he went on to make it worse, 'I'm only thinking about it. I've got loads of ideas. Maybe I'll start a business. Buying and selling stuff.'

'D'you know what you are?' Coggie said, stopping to find her purse as the conductor came along.

'I'll get them,' Alex insisted. He paid, took the tickets and faced her. 'What am I then?'

'You're a—'

'A good guy?'

'A dreamer. That's what. Just like Nathan. His head's in the clouds. He keeps getting sacked from jobs. He cannae concentrate on nothing except his paintings. That's why my daddy takes him to sell that newspaper... to get him out for a while, away from the smelly lock-up.'

'At least he's doing what he enjoys.'

'My parents are always arguing over him. He's turning into a hermit and my daddy thinks it's all my mammy's fault for building his hopes of being an artist. A pot artist or a piss artist, my daddy says. I've got to listen to them arguing about him every night.'

Alex wanted to tell her about his own parents, but she would not have known too much about his dead brother and he would have to explain it all. That could lead to admitting that he spoke to Peter sometimes. Speaking to a dead guy would sound weird. Could be a disaster if he said anything about it.

'Nathan's like a best mate,' he said. 'I like him. Treats you like you're the same age. Knows loads of stuff about music and lends me his albums... Rory Gallagher *Live in Europe*, pure magic.'

'He's my best buddy too but I cannae stand that freaky Pink Floyd music he plays. Don't know why he even listens to it.'

Back in Hardridge, they walked arm in arm to the steps at her door and stood facing each other in the shadows. Alex had thought about this moment for weeks and wanted to tell her how much he liked being with her. Now was he stuck for words, and to make things worse, he trembled a bit. He hoped to God that she didn't notice. She didn't seem to. She raised her chin and pressed close to him.

He placed his hands on her waist and they kissed. It could have lasted longer but for the clicking of paws on the steps.

Homeless came up beside them, sniffed around and then turned and wandered off in the night.

'He didn't bark.'

'He knows us. He smelt us.'

'He barks at nothing sometimes, chasing ghosts,' she said. She kissed him again and then skipped up to her door. 'My daddy says I've not to be standing out here. I've to invite you in.'

Alex showed his face to her parents who were watching telly in the living room, answered their questions about the film and refused a cup of tea. Coggie said they were going through to her room to play records, and Mister Coghlin ordered her to leave her door open.

Coggie closed it. 'Treats me like a baby, so he does.'

She flicked through a stack of albums on the floor, picked out the Jacksons, set it on the record player, then squatted on the bed facing him. 'Who do you like best, the Jacksons or the Osmonds?'

'The Osmonds? Don't think so somehow.'

'Who's best? The Beatles or the—'

'The Stones.'

'What about those boys in town? They were a laugh, sure they were?' she said.

'Aye, but I don't like smarmy show-offs, like Haw.'

'Me neither. Jamie Bryce does that too. Always trying to big himself up. I don't know what Lorna sees in him.'

'Jamie's okay once you get to know him.'

'D'you think we'll still know each other when we're old, like forty?'

'That's yonks away. See when you think about it, Coggie. My ma isnae even forty, she's isnae even thirty-five.'

'I'm gonni ask you to call me Shona from now on. Shona's better, don't you think?'

'Sure Coggie, it's much better,' Alex said, smiling.

'What's the best thing that's ever happened to you?' she asked.

He thought about that for a moment. 'The best would be getting out of hospital... aye, definitely.'

'What would be the worst?'

He wouldn't change his mind about telling her about Peter or his mother. 'The worst? That'll be when the priest caught me stealing from the collection plate. Money that was supposed to be for the starving babies... I didnae really nick it. I was having second thoughts but going by the look on the priest's face you'd have thought I'd eaten all the baby food in the world. Binnie stopped me in the corridor at school. Told me it was a mortal sin that'll scar my soul forever, that I'd roast in hell for it.'

'Oh. She's a right bundle of joy.'

'I denied it.'

'Of course.'

'What about you? What's the best and what's the worst?'

They sat talking like that until around half-ten when her father shouted through saying it was about time Alex was heading home.

Ceylon Tea Centre

Alex's money stretched to a Ben Sherman shirt, a pair of jeans and loafers, the first time he had bought his own clothes, and without his parents' say-so. He wanted to look smart like the older teenagers. Jamie had loads more to spend. He put a deposit on a made-to-measure suit in Burton's, bought a gold neck chain for Lorna, a birthday present, and paid for an application for a provisional driving license at the post office, adding two years to his date of birth. Money came easily to him. At the amusement arcade, he used a small screwdriver to force a gap on the coin-return of a slot machine. He straightened a paper clip and slipped it inside, hitting a trigger that kept paying out until the tube was empty. He half-emptied another machine before the attendant got suspicious over the nonstop clanking of falling coins.

Outside, the wind was swirling up the rain, whipping it sideways into the bus shelters and doorways where people crowded for cover. Alex and Jamie ran with their shopping bags over their heads and turned into HMV in Union Street. Jamie picked out an LP sleeve, *The Who, Live at Leeds,* took it to the sales counter and showed the girl he was holding a fiver. When she bent down for the album, he swapped it for a pound. She didn't notice the switch, took the note and gave him three pounds and fifteen pence in change.

Back on the street, he shoved a handful of coins and a pound note into Alex's pocket. 'You need to watch it with that one, mate. It only works half the time and some people get totally pissed off.'

'Just don't do it when I'm with you. My face is still beaming.'

Shona noticed them as soon as they stepped inside the Ceylon Tea Centre. She was in a waitress uniform and her hair was bundled below a frilly netted cap.

'Table for two?' she said politely.

'You sure it's okay?' Alex asked.

'Walk this way.'

'Need high heels to walk that way,' said Jamie.

They swiped rain from the shoulders of their denim jackets as they followed her to an upstairs table. It was set with tablecloths and napkins and oversized cutlery.

Jamie twirled a fork round his fingers. 'Classy place, eh?'

She looked at the shopping bags. 'Did you win the pools or something? Buy anything nice?'

'Wait to you see this,' Jamie said, taking the jewellery box from his inside pocket and showing-off the gold chain. 'It's for Lorna. Don't say nothing. It's gonni be a surprise.'

'That's pretty,' Shona said, and turned to take an order from a group of silver-haired ladies.

'Listen, Jamie. I've been thinking about the mansion.'

'So have I.'

'I'll go first. I was thinking we could get a boat and row it up the river It'll save us from having to humph the big stuff.'

'What big stuff? Has that grandfather clock taken your fancy?' Jamie didn't wait for an answer, he guessed. 'Hold on, mate. A famous painting? I don't think so. The insurance cops will be onto it and we'll never get it shifted.'

Shona set down a three-tier plate stand. Cream cakes on top, scones in the middle, brown-bread sandwiches and salad underneath. 'Famous paintings and insurance cops. You're a right pair, you two,' she said and carried on serving other customers.

Jamie held a lettuce leaf, sniffed it and let it drop, before stuffing a pineapple cake into his mouth.

Alex, his mouth full of sponge, mumbled, 'Tastes a lot nicer when you get it for free, sure it does?' He wiped crumbs from his lips. 'You got a better idea?'

'Any idea is better than a boat, and better than nicking a daft painting... unless we shove it in fat-face's cellar and call the polis, ha ha.'

'I want it, Jamie.'

'Where are you gonni magic-up this boat from?'

'A raft then? We could build one.'

'Bikes could come in handy. We could cycle the long way to the park, round by Sheep Park cottage, sneak past that polis place.'

'The dog training ground! Are you off your nut? I think I fancy my idea better.'

'We'll use duffel bags. They'll no miss a few wee things since they don't know half of what they've got in them crates, but they'll spot a missing painting straight off. Especially if it's the best one they've got.'

Alex shook his head. 'Nah. They won't. Nathan's already painting a fake for us.'

'Look, it'd be a right good laugh if we could swap it, but it's worth naff all. I'm telling you, mate.'

'Are you gen-up about breaking in? I mean, serious, or—'

'I'm serious. I know a lane in the Gorbals where we can hide the stuff. There's loose stones in the wall. You can move them and crawl inside. I used to hide my scrap metal in there.'

'How do you suppose we get it to the Gorbals... on the bus?'

'What's wrong with that?'

'You kidding? McPeat got stopped and searched three times just for carrying a suitcase... it was full of dirty washing he was taking to the laundry for his ma.'

'We could bury it in the park until we're ready to shift it.'

'What about under the turntable like before? That could be good.'

'We'd need to watch out for the railway workers.'

When Alex saw Shona returning with a pot of tea, he dug into his shopping. 'Nearly forgot,' he said, presenting her with a Barbie doll. 'It's the latest. Princess Barbie.'

She blushed. 'You can be a big diddy sometimes, trying to embarrass me. I'll keep it for my wee cousin.' She tucked it in her apron and began clearing tables.

Jamie let out a laugh. 'I think she wants you to get her something more grown up.'

'She likes Barbies. I've seen stacks of them in her room.'

'I've still got stacks of Lego under my bed, doesnae mean I still play with it.'

'Aye. I suppose.'

Jamie leaned forward, 'We better watch what we're saying from now on. You know, ears and that. We don't talk about the mansion except in the howf, okay?'

'The howf it is.'

'One last thing. Maybe we could build a raft. Try it and see if it's any good. It might be okay. I like your thinking... who's gonni see us on the river at night? Naebody, that's who.'

Alex poured tea, supped it and spat it back in the cup. 'Hot water knocked stupid!' he said. 'Let's go back to the shops. I think you're right. I need to get her something better. Can I tap you for some extra cash if I need it?'

'Nae bother, mate.'

In her house that evening, Alex made an excuse for the Barbie, saying it was only a joke, then gave her the silver charm bracelet that he'd bought in Beaverbrooks. She was thrilled with it. She wore it on their dates and bought trinkets to hang from it — a Scotty Dog, a St Christopher and a small book that opened like a locket and had a photo of her daddy inside.

Dracula was their second movie and the third *Murder on the Orient Express*, both crap compared to *The Godfather*. Still, they enjoyed the cafe afterwards, sitting by the window, a bottle of Coke each and a plate of chips to share. It was a buzz being with her, and to think she enjoyed having him around too. She asked him to meet her every Saturday when she finished work, just so they could walk round the shops and travel home together.

Raft

As much as Alex liked meeting Shona outside the Tea Centre, he got fed up bussing into town every weekend, and was relieved when she was having time off at the September holiday weekend. She suggested they go to the ice skating with Rita, but he had other plans. He was keen to try out the raft-building idea.

That Saturday, the first dry day for weeks, was a good time for raiding the college construction site. It was deserted, apart from the old watchie, who caused a scare when he tottered from his hut as Alex, Forbes, Jamie and McPeat were dragging scaffolding planks through the sticky clay.

'Ho, Watchie! Any chance of a hand with this lot?' Jamie shouted.

'That's what you're paid for,' the watchie mumbled. He took a pee and went back inside.

The added weight of the wet clay meant they couldn't carry a plank each, so they paired up and carried one between two.

Shona and Rita were at the bus stop on the opposite side of the road as they paraded past with the planks across their shoulders. Shona called out to them, 'Look who's been playing in the mud like a bunch of schoolboys.'

Jamie, Forbes and McPeat turned their heads, waiting for Alex to reply to the dig.

Unable to think of anything better to say, he said, 'But we are schoolboys!'

McPeat tried to back him up. 'I suppose you think you're a big woman, Coggie Coghlin.'

'Grow up, McPeat. And my name's Shona if you don't mind.'

'And mine's Mister McPeat if you don't mind.'

The boys laughed and walked on.

'I want to speak with you, Alex Hannah.'

'Wow, proper names! It must be serious.'

'Shut it, Bryce,' she yelled.

Alex laid down his end of the plank and met her halfway, on the grass verge. 'What are you getting all crabby for?'

'What are you hanging around with him for?'

'Who?'

'You know who. He stole cutlery from my work. I could've got sacked.'

'I didnae see him.'

'You're not like him. You shouldnae go near him or you'll get a bad name. People are blaming him for breaking into houses.'

'It isnae him doing that.'

The others were watching as she stood, tight lipped, arms crossed. She squinted at the mud on his shoes and trousers. 'Go and get changed and come with us. We'll wait for you.'

'Hurry, Shona. The bus is coming,' Rita shouted.

Haw and a few of his cronies, holding ice hockey boots, were bumping their way to the front of the queue.

'I'll go with you next week,' he said.

'I'm working next week.'

She made her way back to Rita.

As they carried the planks through the path in the woods, Jamie said, 'You better watch out for Haw.'

'How come?'

'I heard he's chasing her.'

'Lots of people fancy her. Anyway, she hates him.'

'What, even more than she hates me?'

'Nah, I think you win on that one, Jamie. You shouldnae have stolen from her work.'

'What are you on about, mate? I didnae.'

They dumped the planks at the riverbank, keeping well back from the edge because the river was full to the brim and running silent. The bank was crumbling into the muddy water and foaming whirlpools were appearing and disappearing among the debris being swept downstream — broken trees, leaves, plastic bags, beer bottles, footballs, even a sheep with bulging dead eyes on its bloated head. The boys watched it float past and did not chuck stones at it.

'Did you see them eyes? I'll get nightmares the night,' McPeat said.

'Me an all,' Forbes added. 'I thought sheep could swim. Can sheep no swim?'

'That one cannae,' Alex said.

Half an hour later and they were back in the street, using McPeat's penknife to cut lines of washing rope from the back gardens. Next, they raided the railway dump and rolled away empty oil drums taking them across the ash flats and over the golf course fairways, baffling and angering the golfers.

After lashing the oil drums to the planks, the raft was ready to be tried-out. But they didn't dare. The river was too scary. Anyway, the air smelt rotten and was nipping with horseflies, not a good time to be hanging around. They dragged the raft under the wild rhubarb bushes and left it there.

By Monday the river had sunk back, leaving ribbons of litter flapping in the overhanging branches. It was still running fast, although much slower than before.

The boys were pulling on the raft when a chubby brown rat scurried through the reeds.

'Killer rats!' McPeat said, dancing around as if it was at his feet. 'Go straight for your throat so they do. We better get, before it comes back with its pals.'

Forbes nudged him. 'It's only a water vole that's been flooded out its nest.'

'Forget the rat-vole or whatever it is... let's see how this thing floats,' Jamie said.

The others got with him, pushing the raft, panting in the clammy air as they inched it over the reeds and into the water. It bobbed up and down like a cork. They tied one end of line to it. The other end they tied to a tree with enough slack to reach the opposite bank.

Jamie lifted a washed-up stick. 'I've got the paddle, so I'll go first.' After stripping to his pants, he squatted on the raft and planted the stick on the riverbed, pushing off. The flow caught hold quickly, taking the raft to the end of the line, stopping it with a jolt. As it wobbled from side to side, he prodded for the riverbed trying to steady himself, but the water was too deep. The stick and his arm disappeared under the surface, causing the raft to tumble and ditch him over the side.

Slipping around laughing, the others took a while to realise that he was struggling. Each time he tried to pull himself up, the raft tumbled, leaving him gasping. He held on as they tried to haul it back. They couldn't. Not against the flow, but their efforts caused it to swing round on the end of the line, hitting the bank.

Jamie clambered over it and out of the water. He winced as he dabbed the scratches and welts on his arms. 'We need to stop it bouncing around so much,' he said. 'We should weigh it down with something.'

They anchored it to a tree and went scouring the bank for boulders.

On reaching the clearing at the rope swing they met Grogan and Cammy Sinclair. Cammy walked straight up to them. 'Alright, lads?' he said, sounding happy to see them.

The boys didn't answer. They were staring at the commando knife that Grogan was using to sharpen a stick. It was ten times the size of McPeat's penknife — the same scary knife he had pulled on Alex over a year ago. He passed it slowly through the reeds to let them see how sharp it was. The reeds didn't bend, they toppled, sliced through as if by a razor. He took aim and threw it at the oak tree, trying to make it stick in the bark, but it hit sideways and tumbled through the air. Everyone scattered, tripping over each other to get out of its way.

Grogan lifted it and pretended to pick his fingernails with it.

'Put it away or you'll cut yourself and go greeting to your mammy,' Forbes said.

It wasn't wise to be winding-up that nutter, especially when he had a knife in his hand. Alex gave his brother an angry stare, then tried to win Grogan over. 'We're building a raft. You for helping?'

Grogan looked at him, then at Jamie. He slid the knife into a leather sheath on his belt and said, 'Okay. But if I get any hassle, I'm letting it loose.'

'This could be trouble,' Jamie whispered to Alex.

'I know.'

They carried boulders and lashed them to the sides of the raft until it sat low in the water. It was steadier now, the river slurping around the oil drums, but it would be no use for the mansion house job, and Alex knew it.

He spoke to Jamie. 'We won't get it up the river for a start. We'll end up in the drink.'

'Aye. Imagine trying to swim in there in the dark. Them rat-voles chewing your balls off. Forget it, mate.'

To Alex, the antiques were still worth thinking about. They might even fetch enough to buy a house, somewhere well away from the social workers. Yet the painting felt more important. His mind wouldn't let it go. He had made excellent progress in finding a canvas and getting Nathan to start work on it, but he wasn't up for swapping it on his own. He needed Jamie's help.

Jamie stopped Forbes from getting on the raft. 'The river's too fast for you.'

'I'm a better swimmer than you any day,' Forbes said, trying to push him aside.

At that moment, Alex sensed a sudden change in the air. The hairs on the back of his neck were standing on edge. He looked up and saw rooks and starlings swooping from the darkening clouds into the trees. He got hold of his brother, gripping his arm. 'Jamie's right.'

They were beginning to wrestle when Grogan crawled aboard. 'Too late,' he said, shoving off.

Sure enough, lightning frazzled the sky seconds later, followed by rumbling thunder right above their heads, then thick straight rain. It clapped on the mud and bounced off the river, big plopping ripples.

Grogan tried like mad to pull the raft along the line, and Cammy Sinclair moved to help, but Jamie stopped him. They took cover under the trees with the others.

'Get me in,' Grogan shouted.

'That's serious rain,' McPeat said.

'No messing with that rain.'

'Get me in ya bastards!'

'What's up, feart of thunder?'

'Nowt to worry about. It's just God moving his furniture.'

'Maybe he's angry with you.'

'Get me in or I'll plunge the lot of you!'

Alex took the penknife from McPeat, unfolded it and held it against the line. He puffed out his cheeks and spoke like the guy in *The Godfather*. 'Does fat-face sleep with the fishes?'

'Why not?' said Jamie.

'Aye, why not?' said Forbes.

'I'll fuckin kill you, Hannah!'

Stretched tight, the anchor line snapped easily as soon as Alex put pressure on the penknife.

'Enjoy your trip to the sea.'

Grogan floated away quietly, trying to keep the raft steady as it seesawed and swirled round the bend.

His tale did its round on the street. He drifted on the River Cart, halfway through Pollok, and could've ended up going down the Clyde if a fallen tree hadn't snagged the raft. He waded chest-deep to the bank but kept sliding back into the water on account of the mud, so he waded further along, to where the bank was thick with giant hogweed. With his knife, he cut his way to the top, slicing the plants and using the stumps for handholds. There was no pain, not then. The agony came later that night, burning and blistering on his hands, arms and neck. His mother called a taxi and took him to Accident and Emergency at two in the morning. In the days and weeks that followed, he showed-off his hogweed scars and made big announcements about killing the bastards who'd caused them.

Trainers

While everyone else was at school, Jamie was on the golf course hunting for lost golf balls to earn a few extra pennies. Alex took the day off to try it, and to get Jamie's thoughts on the mansion house. Their shoes, socks and the bottoms of their jeans were drenched after searching the rain-soaked grass, and with a couple of dozen balls weighing down their Parka pockets, they called it quits and waited on the fifth tee for the lone golfer who was hacking his way down the fairway.

Jamie was harping on about Lorna. He was planning to surprise her with the gold chain at a family birthday party on Friday. She lived in a bought-house in Ralston, sang in a church choir, was a member of a hill-walking group and had applied to train as a nurse when she left school, which meant she'd be moving to live in the nurses' quarters on Great Western Road.

The golfer was taking an age to find his ball among the fallen leaves, and the Jamie and Lorna story was rambling on too long.

'Take a breather,' Alex said.

Jamie leant on the fence and cracked his knuckles. 'What's up with your coupon?'

'Nothing... I was wondering. The antiques. We ever gonni go for them?'

'I could use the money, mate, learn to drive, take Lorna on trips and that. Then again, it's iffy with the alarms, plus the crates could've been moved by now. There's easier places to tan.'

'I'll do it myself if you're backing down.'

'You huvnae got what it takes.'

'And you have?'

'I'm no backing down.'

'So, is it gonni happen?'

'Aye.'

'When?'

'Soon.'

'When's soon?'

'No yet.'

The golfer reached the green, the ball getting inches from the pin on his third putt. He lifted it and stepped up to the tee, his waterproof jacket and trousers squeaking.

'Golf balls going cheap, Spalding and Dunlops,' Jamie announced and held out a selection in his cupped hands.

Ignoring him, the golfer let his bag slip from his shoulder, took out a club and teed-up.

'Have a peek. Not a nick on any,' Jamie said.

'This is private property. You've no right being on it, let alone touting golf balls.'

'We're no causing any bother. What's it to you anyhow?'

'Vice-captain, that's what.'

Jamie put the golf balls on the ground and added more from his pockets. 'See for yourself. None of your cheap Pollok spuds. Superior Haggs Castle balls, all of them. All guaranteed to go two hundred yards straight down the middle, and vice-captains are entitled to discount. Half a dozen for fifty pence.'

'Not short on sales patter are you, son?' said the vice-captain. He peered at the balls, picked out six and paid for them, put them in his bag and got set to hit the teed-up ball. He stood over it, shifting his hands and feet before raising the club, holding it over his head for far too long, as if he was stuck. Then a wild chopping swipe that sent the ball spinning towards the cow field.

He cursed, shook his head and teed-up another, going through the same routine, this time hitting a low runner that pulled up in the carpet of soggy leaves. 'I've been thinking of splashing out on a new set of John Letters,' he said, inspecting the head of his club as if it was the club's fault.

'Why don't you try a slow smooth swing like the good players?' Jamie said.

'How would you know what good players do?'

'From watching. I'm on here a lot.'

'Don't you two have better things to do with your time like school or work?'

'If it's new clubs you're needing, my mate gets them half price, straight from the warehouse.'

The vice-captain shouldered his bag. 'I'm on the course every Monday morning if you want to let me see them. Although, don't make the mistake of thinking I want to buy anything illegal. I'll need to see a receipt.'

Jamie tried to talk Alex into going to check out the sports shop near Central Station. Alex had walked past it a few times. There was no end of sport's kit in the window — golf, football, rugby, archery, darts, even curling.

'Nah,' Alex decided, remembering the trouble with the Mancinis.

'What's up, you lost your bottle?'

'Aye. Like you with the mansion. All talk, no action.'

'Suit yourself.'

'I will.'

'I'd forget about the mansion if I were you, mate.'

'How come?'

'I'm no saying we couldnae do it, we could, we might. It's too much of a risk right now.'

'What? Trying to nick golf clubs from the middle of town... that isnae risky somehow?'

'It'll be a doddle. I'll ask McPeat.'

'It's penny pinching compared with the antiques.'

'At least there's nae alarms to figure out.'

The plan for the sports shop sounded simple — McPeat creates a distraction and Jamie strolls off with the clubs. And it worked, for Jamie stepped off the train with a golf bag full of them.

He told Alex and Forbes about it while they waited for McPeat to return. Signs were good from the start. The tracksuited salesman acted as if he owned the place and looked like he would give chase. That's what they wanted. The only problem, he also looked fit. McPeat wasn't put off. He was game for anything, badly needing new shoes and faster than anyone. He asked for Adidas Samba, size five, letting the salesman see the readies, pretending to count out the pound notes like Jamie had told him. He tried them for fit and walked in them for a better feel, towards the door, then bolted when Jamie opened it. The salesman barged past Jamie and tore up West Nile Street, close on McPeat's heels. As customers hurried out to see the action, Jamie stepped in amongst the window display, added a Dunlop driver and a three-wood to the full set of clubs that were already in the golf bag, saw there was room for more, added an air rifle and stuffed four rugby jerseys inside the zipped pockets. He walked out with it slung over his shoulder.

The tale had just about finished, when McPeat jumped from the bus. He spotted the boys and pointed to his Adidas Sambas, a grin lighting up his face.

Jamie gave him a shoulder hug. 'I thought you'd been nabbed, wee man. You should've seen that nutter's face, veins sticking out like he was taking a flaky.'

'I nearly did get nabbed. Chased me all the way onto the Kingston Bridge, so he did. Had to shimmy doon scaffolding tubes, so I did. Made me scuff my new trainers, the scumbag. Lucky for me he was feart of heights. What did you get?'

'At least sixty quid's worth. They're in my cellar. We can flog—'

Jamie backflipped over the hedge.

Mister Grogan had been on the bus and was staggering towards them. All six feet four of him, almost blocking the light from the streetlamp, big round face and rolling eyes like his sons.

He grabbed a handful of Alex's shirt. 'Where's Bryce?' he growled.

Alex looked around as if searching. 'No here,' he said, and turned to Forbes, copying the gruff voice, 'Where's Bryce?'

'No here,' Forbes answered putting on the same voice, then looked to McPeat. 'Where's Bryce?'

McPeat's Mister Grogan impression was best. 'No here,' he croaked.

Alex's shirt ripped as the man twisted it upwards, trying to lift him.

'You don't like that, eh? Not so fuckin smart now are you, eh? You're a chancer like your slimy thieving mate. He's gonni learn just how fuckin dumb it is to go breaking into folks' hooses.'

'Hoi,' McPeat said. 'Are you Phil Grog-on's old man?'

'What of it?'

'Deserves you right, ha ha.'

Mister Grogan swung for him, wobbling like a skittle as McPeat danced around.

'You couldnae catch a cold, whisky breath.'

'The height of shite, the lot of youse. Youse are for it, my sons are gonni fuckin burst youse.'

'Your sons couldnae burst a wet paper bag,' Forbes said from a safe distance.

'I'll break your fuckin skull.'

'Please don't beat him with the big stick master,' McPeat said in a high-pitched baby voice.

'Wee bastards! I know where you live.'

The boys howled in mock fear.

After the man staggered up the road cursing and growling, Jamie clambered through the hedge.

'I've never tanned a hoose. Honest. Sure I huvnae, Alex? Tell them it's isnae me.'

'We believe you, Jamie, thousands wouldnae,' McPeat said.

'If they think it's me, I'm gonni get done in.'

Nabbed

Things started to go wrong for Jamie and McPeat when they were with Alex in Mitchell Street Snooker Hall. McPeat in his stride had rattled in a break of forty-eight, reds and blacks, going strong and drawing an audience to the edge of the light. Alex wasn't bothered about not getting a shot. He hoped McPeat would clear the table and impress everyone. A legend. He lowered his head and listened while McPeat took on a difficult long pot. He liked doing that, waiting to hear the clack-clack followed by the rattle of the ball in the pocket.

Instead, he heard, 'Hey buddy!'

A man in a white shirt, crew cut hair, had stepped into the column of light. 'Can I borrow your rest stick? Ours is missing.'

McPeat scowled at him. 'What's the fuck's the matter with you, can you no see I'm in the middle of a break here?'

'Aye, you're right out of order there, big man,' said a spectator.

McPeat kept scowling as he lifted the rest from the hooks at the side of the table. 'You've disturbed my flow, so you have. Here, take the fuckin thing!'

'Sorry,' the man said, reaching over the table for it.

Chalking his cue, Jamie edged round the table and nodded to Alex to move in, then spoke in McPeat's ear. 'That guy, he's eyeing your watch.'

McPeat was bent over the table, cueing up. He turned his head to the side. 'Eh?'

Alex had paid little attention to McPeat's watch, a chunky, metal bracelet type.

'He's iffy,' Jamie said. 'I mean, what's a rest stick? Who the fuck calls it that? I'm sure I've seen him somewhere. Could be from one of the photos at the cricket club. We should bolt.'

'What cricket club?' Alex asked.

'Wait till I'm finished. I'm blitzing my record here.'

'I'm off, wee man. You better come an all. Alex, you stay here. Hit a few shots. Make like you're waiting for us. You've nowt to worry about.'

McPeat laid the cue on the cloth and followed Jamie, mumbling, 'Far too edgy, that's your problem.'

Alex picked it up wondering what to do and decided not to hang around. He put it back on the table and caught up with his pals in Mitchell Lane.

Walking fast, they were soon on the pedestrian bridge, crossing the Clyde to the Gorbals, with McPeat still moaning about his snooker break. 'I could've cleared the table, so I could. That guy didnae even see my watch.'

'You cannae miss it! Wearing it halfway up your arm like that.'

'It's too big for my wrist. Anyway, I don't try to tell you how to wear things, do I? I can wear it how I like.'

'What's this about a cricket club?' Alex asked again.

The bridge shook.

Two cops on massive horses were pounding towards them.

Without breaking step, McPeat let the watch slip from his wrist and dropkicked it into the river. Just in time, for they were on him in seconds. They each grabbed a handful of his denim jacket and lifted him clean off the ground between the horses.

Jamie, with his back against the railings, stuffed money down the inside of his pants. There was no point in running — a squad van was blocking the bridge at the Carlton Place end.

A spotty rookie and a big sergeant bundled them into it, onto a wooden bench next to a sleeping piss-smelling drunk, then climbed in after them.

'Where is it?' the rookie said, poking McPeat in the chest.

McPeat held up his foot. 'I'm gonni need to sue that horse, so I am. Stood on my toe, so it did. Broke it, so it did.'

The rookie slapped him across the ear. 'Where's the watch, fly man?'

'Who you calling fly man, pizza face?'

Another slap, harder this time.

'That isnae even sore,' McPeat said, gritting his teeth. His eyes were watering.

'Empty your pockets.'

Fumbling around, McPeat fished out a packet of chewing gum and his penknife.

'An offensive weapon, that's six months for a start.'

Alex turned out seventy pence and a broken pencil, Jamie a set of keys.

'Explain the keys?'

'Hoose. Cellar. Bike. Nae crime in that.'

'Thieving a Rolex is a crime.'

'What's a Rolex?'

The sergeant ogle-eyed them one at a time. 'Been in bother before?'

'No me,' said Jamie.

'No me,' said McPeat.

Alex's voice let him down, going high and wobbly like a wee kid about to cry, 'No me,' he squeaked.

Jamie and McPeat, giggling, let their heads drop.

'I've seen your ugly mugshots. I think you lot have gone and mugged that poor soul who's in intensive care fighting for his life. You're for the high jump.'

'You've been watching too much telly,' said McPeat.

The sergeant took out his notebook. 'We'll soon find out who's got a record and who hasn't. Name, date of birth and address?' He jotted down their details, slid open the door, stepped out and spoke into his walkie-talkie. A few minutes passed before he returned. 'Right, you, baby face, out!'

Jamie and McPeat couldn't stop laughing now.

'Cuff the two numpties.'

The sergeant stood on the pavement, staring down his nose at Alex as if waiting for a confession.

'You could be let off with a warning if you tell me what they did with the watch.'

'I don't know about any watch, honest, officer.'

The sergeant eyed him a while longer.

'It's the truth.'

'You're on our records now. If you're involved, we'll have you jailed so fast you'll think you've got a rocket up your arse. You hear?'

Alex nodded.

'On your way.'

Alex looked back when he heard the van driving off with his pals inside.

With no word on them for days, he knocked on the Bryces' door. After inviting him into the kitchen, Jamie's granny slumped on a chair and put her arm to her forehead. 'It's too much at my age. My heart's roasted with that boy.'

He took the other chair, facing her.

'He's been remanded until the case is called. I've been to see him. He thinks he's too smart for them. Thinks they've got no proof, but they ransacked this place, emptied the drawers, tipped over the mattresses, tossed everything from the wardrobes and found what they were hunting for — savings stamps that he'd been hiding under the cabinet and a gold chain in the pocket of his jacket. They called me an old hag and threatened to lock me up for saying they were mine.'

'Jamie bought that chain, I was with him, honest, Missus Bryce.'

'He paid for it with dirty money, money from thieving. It's the same thing.'

'He's been collecting golf balls and selling them.'

'They're claiming the gold chain was stolen from a jewellery shop break-in and the savings stamps from the post office. Jamie's fingerprints were all they needed. I'm sick to my bones with all of this. God knows what'll become of him.'

Alex couldn't hide his embarrassment at his attempt to mislead. She knew Jamie far better than he did.

'They raided McPeat's place too,' she said. 'They've charged his ma's fancy man for handling stolen goods. He's out on bail. It's far better treatment than the boys got. That place could destroy them. I'm praying for them.'

'Is there anything I can do, Missus Bryce?'

'Please go and see Jamie. Talk to him. Tell him to own up. They've promised he'll get probation if he does.'

Scuffs

It was an hour and a half by bus, train and another bus, passing miles of frost-covered fields before road signs to the remand home began to appear. The remaining passengers were now talking openly about the place, visiting mammies and grannies, grumbling that it was set in the middle of nowhere just to make it difficult for them, especially in this freezing weather.

They got off the bus when it pulled up beyond a notice, *HRM Remand Institution. Access for Authorised Business Only*. The gate next to it was open and the dry-stone wall on either side was topped with a single line of barbed wire.

Hunched against the piercing cold Alex followed the group of visitors, shortcutting from the path across a playing field to the main building. With its long windows and turret, you could mistake it for a church rather than a remand home.

A man in an anorak blocked his way and said nothing.

Alex showed his visitor's pass.

Anorak-man could've been in his late twenties, could've been much older, it was hard to tell on account of his drawn-in face and bald head that was partly disguised with long strands of combed-over hair. He nodded to the waiting area but moved aside only an inch or so. Alex squeezed through.

The visitors, when a bell sounded, shuffled along a wood-panelled corridor that was covered in scuffmarks from years of inmate traffic. It led to an assembly room where boys sat behind tables, their eyes searching for relatives.

Jamie stood so that Alex could pick him out. He was in the same loose-fitting outfit as the others, faded grey denim shirt and jeans, white sandshoes. 'Hey, mate,' he said, beckoning to the empty seat.

Anorak-man and another man were standing against the wall with their arms folded, watching.

'Cold enough, eh?' Jamie said.

'No half. The radio said minus nine last night.'

'Reminds me of Coggie's joke about brass monkeys. Chink chink.'

'Good one.'

Jamie's right hand was swollen and bruised. He noticed Alex looking at it.

'I punched the wall.'

'You punched the wall?'

'Aye.'

'What did the wall do to you?'

'I put a big dent in the plaster. That comb-over pervert made me stand facing it for four hours, barefooted on the stone-cold floor. Fuckin torture, mate.'

'How's McPeat doing?'

'I don't see much of the wee man. A battle axe of a nurse gave us a medical. I heard her saying he was to be put in with the bruisables, whatever that means.'

After a quiet moment, Jamie said, 'You seen Lorna?'

'Just in passing, at school.'

'She writes. She wants to visit but I won't let her. I don't want her to see me in this place.'

'It's a trek to get here.'

'I know. My granny said that. She sat in that chair cradling her handbag and crying for an hour.'

'She says you've to own up.'

Jamie sucked through his teeth and shook his head. 'Listen, I'll tell you how it works. Own up to anything and get done for everything. That's how.'

'You got a lawyer?'

'Don't see him doing much good. They cannae touch me on the gold chain but I'm shitting myself over the post office. Her royal majesty's post office, they called it in court. They say I could get five years for that. A fuckin death sentence it'll seem like.'

'They telt your granny that you could get off with probation.'

'Lying bastards. That's those two detectives who interviewed me. The pally one pats me on the shoulder and says

I've left my prints everywhere, then says he can report that I've co-operated, and he'll drop the charges on the cricket club, but only if I save them the bother of a trial and own up to the post office, the jewellers and the hooses. Honest mate, I've never broken into any hooses neither I have, or any jewellers. And there cannae be any fingerprints cause I always wear gloves.'

'You should've telt me about the cricket club.'

'I didnae want to drag you in.'

'You should've telt me anyhow.'

'It was a bad move. Nowt for nicking except a few bottles of booze, a couple of packets of cigars and that daft watch. I didnae have a clue it was pure valuable. Worth a few grand and it's rusting away at the bottom of the Clyde.'

'D'you think they'll want to talk to me, y'know, since I got booked and that? I'm scared they'll come to my door.'

'Nah. It's us they're after. They've been holding mine's and McPeat's description. The other tec, the stone-faced one, he punches me in the guts, twice. The first winded me and the second came before I could catch my breath. That'll give me something to think about he says as I'm lying there puking.'

'That's assault.'

'As if he cares. Says they can put me in borstal as soon as I'm sixteen. That's fuckin scary an all, mate. They can keep topping up your sentence in borstal. Break any rules and you end up getting an extra six months. Even if you toe the line, they'll accuse you of something if they don't like your face.'

Alex glanced around. 'What are they all in for?'

'You name it. Offensive weapons, arson, shop lifting, breaking and entering. Some have been in homes and approved schools all of their lives.'

'They raided McPeat's hoose, y'know?'

'Aye. I know.'

'What about Coggie?'

'What about her?'

'Did you tell her about me getting nicked?'

'Nah, nothing.'

'I don't want her to know.'

'It'll be the talk of the street soon enough.'

'Aye.'

Another silence.

'How's Nathan getting on with that painting?'

'He keeps saying it cannae be rushed.'

'You best forget about it.'

'Aye.'

'How's you mammy doing?'

'Alright. A wee bit bothered now and again… but alright. How's the grub in here?'

'Shit. Everything's shit. The grub, the bunk, the freezing cold dribbling showers, the weirdos, and the boys that think they're gangsters. A few are. You wouldnae want to get on their wrong side. But some cry in their beds. I heard one getting dragged along the corridor the other night, sobbing *amsorryamsorryamsorry*. It's all shit.'

'It sounds it.'

'Guess what's worse?'

Alex didn't have to guess. He knew from his time in hospital. 'Feeling like you've been left behind, forgotten about.'

'Aye, right you are, mate.'

During the next bout of silence Alex stared through the window to the snow on the near-by hills.

'You need stories to pass the time in here, mate,' Jamie said, digging his hands deep in his pockets and stretching his legs. 'It keeps you going. Here's one... we're locked below the Sheriff Court and our legal aid lawyer comes in carrying a pile of papers under his arm and asks which one of us is Cornelius. I thought he had the wrong cell, and then McPeat says *that's me*. Can you believe it? Cornelius! What a belter. I didnae know that, did you?'

'Aye. He hates it.'

'Anyway, the lawyer wants to know how we're pleading. We both say, *No guilty*, and he tells us to remember and pronounce our T's in court, so McPeat says, *Note guil-tee.* The lawyer just shakes his head at him. We got remanded for twenty-eight days to give them time to investigate. The lawyer now wants us to plead guilty and says he'll fix a date when the worst judges aren't around. But I'm no waiting. I'm out of here, mate. Doing a runner.'

Alex straightened and leant across the table. 'For real?'

'Sit back, mate. You're drawing attention.'

'It looks easy. You could jump that wall nae bother.'

'I've got a better idea. There's a guy in here, Jake Armstrong, a gargoyle-faced headcase from Shettleston who drinks floor polish to get blotto. He's like the leader of the hard men. I'll pick a fight with him, call him a grassing bawbag. He's bound to do me for that.'

'Then what?'

'Then I play dead.'

'You might be dead by the sounds of it.'

'They take me to hospital and that's when I bolt. Save me from having to find my way back over them country roads.'

'Doesnae sound too clever to me. I'd start thinking of something better if I were you. Something that doesnae involve getting done in.'

The bell rang, chairs screeched, and mammies and grannies began hugging their boys.

'You want me to send you a book or anything?'

'Don't bother. I won't be here.'

'Watch yourself, Jamie.'

'Aye, you too, mate.'

Chucked

Forbes teamed-up with Alex on Friday, collecting both the milk money and paper round money, to save them from double calling. It meant they could finish quicker, and Forbes could get out to the movies with his pals. It worked, but he was too early for his best customer, a woman in Bellahouston Drive who always gave him a giant tip, twice as much as her newspaper bill. Her husband had answered the door that evening, tipping only a few pennies. Forbes said he would need to hang back from now on, until that stingy old git left for the pub. They shared stories of their customers as they walked home, the good tippers, the no tippers, the woman who gave you a boiled sweet, the complainers, the dogs who acted as if they had rabies, snarling and foaming at the mouth — chew your hand off if you put it through the letter box. Forbes fell into his cackling laugh when Alex spoke about Missus Murphy. She had asked him to babysit her kids, one of them being Jimmy Murphy, a boy in Forbes's class.

They were on the peak of the hill at the railway, giggling, when they met Shona and Rita and Haw and Cammy Sinclair coming up the other side.

Shona, her black leather jerkin buttoned to the neck, looked beautiful in her blue eye shadow and glossy red lipstick.

'Alright lads? What are you two up to? Monkey business, I bet.'

Alex couldn't speak. He felt like he'd been kicked in the throat. She'd just let go of Haw's arm. Him standing at her side in his three-inch platform boots and his ginger hair sticking up in a Ziggy Stardust cut.

'Monkey business! Who d'you think you're talking to?' Forbes said, annoyed at her smugness.

'Chill it,' Haw said, facing up to him.

Alex used his elbow to push Haw back. 'Chill it? What the fuck's that meant to mean, Haw-Haw? You think you're a movie star or something?'

'Alex Hannah! Don't you dare try to act the hard man!' Shona yelled, pointing her finger in his face. She pulled Haw onto the stairs of the railway station. The other two followed, Rita turning and shaking her head at Alex, like she was disappointed in him.

'We should go down there and give that Ziggy bastard a kicking,' Forbes said. 'No a wee slap neither. I'm talking black eyes and sore chuckies for months.'

'Shut it, Forbes.'

'Aye, that's right, get mad at me like it's my fault.'

Alex caught Shona glancing up at him from the platform. She turned away quickly.

'I'm only saying, if you keep on fighting people, you'll be the one who ends up getting second prize.'

'You saying I'll end up like this?' Forbes pressed his nose flat to his face then spoke with a nasal squeak. 'Like I've gone ten rounds with Muhammad Ali.'

He kept talking when Alex didn't reply. 'That ginger nut is gonni get a kicking anyhow. Want to know what for? He slagged off our donkey jackets, that's what for.'

Now Forbes was putting on a hurt face and squinting sideways at Alex. 'What's that on your mug? You're dying to laugh. I can tell.'

'Donkey jackets? That was yonks ago,' Alex said, and smiled, hiding his stomach-churning feeling.

'Doesnae make it right, does it? He's had loads of time to say sorry.'

'Ah well, I suppose you've got a point. Haw's due a hiding right enough.'

Nathan, wiping his hands with a rag, said his usual, 'Alright Alex.' His jumper and jeans were paint-splashed like everything else in the lock-up — multicoloured blobs of paint everywhere. The place stank of turps, a one-bar electric fire was glowing below a workbench, a Neil Young track was playing on a cassette recorder and a spotlight was targeted at a painting of two shipyard workers. A photograph of them was pinned to the wall. Alex ducked a painting that hung from the rafters and dodged another two on trestles to reach a beaten-up armchair. He checked it for wet paint and sat in it.

'I suppose you want to know how I'm getting on with the El Greco?'

'Aye, Nathan. I wouldnae mind seeing it.'

'Hold on till I give my welders a wee bit more of a backdrop.'

The men in the painting were old and tough and haggard, yet cheery because of their friendly wrinkled smiles and bright blue eyes, a striking contrast of colour that was Nathan's trademark. He worked his magic, using a flat knife to mix and spread the colours, adding clouds and a crane to the portrait. He stepped back from it. 'It's a commission.'

'How does that go again?'

'It means I've been asked to paint it specially.'

'Like me asking you to paint the El Greco? Is that a commission?'

'You usually get paid for a commission. This is a wee bit different. It's an assignment from you'll never guess who... the head honcho at art school. He's been to see me. He's taking a new job at some art college in London. It's supposed to have a good reputation. He's asked me to paint these two characters and wants me to use it to apply. Says he'll approve my application personally.'

'You're getting scouted like McPeat with Partick Thistle?'

'Something like that.'

'He must know you're good, this honcho guy.'

Nathan wiped his hands again, then scrabbled under the workbench and lifted out a canvas. 'It's only the first few layers,' he said, setting it on the bench for Alex to see.

The image sparked Alex's imagination once more, but it was only a dull outline of the *Lady in a Fur Wrap*.

'There's a fair bit left to do. I should have it ready by March. February if I get stuck in.'

'Nae point in rushing. Take as long as you need.'

'What's the matter? You fed up?'

Alex was more than fed up, he was in a rotten mood.

Nathan lifted a fresh canvas and set it up on the bench, 'Wait and I'll show you something.'

He squinted at Alex a few times while squeezing the paint straight onto the canvas. 'Can you see who it is yet?'

A few squiggly lines of peachy coloured paint were all Alex could see.

'Nah, who is it?'

'It's you.'

'Eh?'

'Don't you think it looks like you?'

'Is it supposed to look like me?'

'Oh. Nearly forgot,' Nathan said, and turned the canvas round. 'Upside-down painting is my party trick.'

Alex immediately recognised himself, drawn as a cartoon character with a petted lip.

'See what I'm saying? You don't create a masterpiece in a rush. It needs to be sculpted, good and proper.'

'I'm not rushing you. It's up to you to say how long it takes.'

'Have you lost heart in your plot to rob the fat capitalists of their prized possession?'

'I still think it could be done.'

'I know it could. I could do it myself if I wanted. I've been back to study it a few times. There's hardly anyone there in the mornings. It'd be dead easy. Unhook it, pins out, canvas out, fake in, pins in, back on the wall and away with it. Job done.'

'As easy as that, eh?'

'Need to be careful not to fold the canvas or roll it too tightly or it'll crease. That'll ruin it.'

Alex sneaked in the only question that he had gone there to ask. 'I noticed Shona at the station earlier, don't suppose you know where she was going?'

'Dunno. Off to the dancing likely, with her wee pal, what's her name, Rhona?'

'Rita.'

Nathan shrugged and screwed up his face. 'Ask her yourself, why don't you?'

He didn't quite say that Alex was being a prick about it, but that's what it felt like, and he was right.

'Aye, I will ask her.'

Swapping Shirts

The constant rain left nothing dry outside and was doing its best to soak the inside too, seeping through the flat roof, causing the damp patches to huddle into one big mouldy patch on the ceiling. Alex gazed at it. He was in the spare bedroom holding one end of a cloth while his mother guided the other end past the needle on the sewing machine, dressmaking for a woman she'd met at the community centre. The doctor had told her she needed to get out more often and had arranged for her to attend that place on Saturday mornings, some sort of Woman's Institute club. It was good for her to be sitting around drinking tea and chatting with people.

She was operating the foot pedal when a whistle sounded in the back garden. Alex stretched and opened the window.

'Meet you in the howf,' said a voice in the dark.

Alex could barely make it out because of the wind and rain, but he knew who it was. He handed the cloth to his mother. 'I need to go out and see my mate for a few minutes.'

'How am I meant to get this finished?'

'Forbes can help, he's doing nothing.'

'Don't go out in that rain, son. It's the kind that soaks you right through to your bones.'

'It's rain, Ma. The same wet kind you always get. I won't be gone for long.'

He grabbed his Parka. Then he was out, hood up, face down against the icy cold smir. A few minutes later and he had clambered into the howf.

'Christ, Jamie. How did you get here?'

Jamie was wrapped up in a sleeping bag. 'Get set for a story and a half,' he said, passing a blanket to Alex.

Alex plonked himself in the car seat, 'Cannae wait.'

'That guy I was telling you about, Jake Armstrong, remember?'

'Gargoyle-features?'

'Aye, the headcase. He was bossing the table tennis when I walks up to him and taps him on the shoulder and calls him a grassing bawbag like I said I would. Next thing I'm on the floor with a bloody mouth and two slack teeth. They took me to get cleaned up. I staggered, said I was dizzy and feeling sick, so they let me lie on my bunk. I was still there at lights-out and still there in the morning, on top of the covers. I didnae budge when the lads tried to wake me. The teachers came and shouted and kicked the bunk and jabbed me in the ribs. I'm telling you, mate, it's the hardest thing to do... to not move when someone's shouting in your lug, poking your ribs and tickling the soles of your feet. You wouldnae believe how hard that is. I listened to them talking, saying there wasn't much in it, a head butt from Armstrong was all.' Jamie touched his two front teeth. 'Aye, right. They're still slack. Anyway, they carried me and laid me on the back seat of a car and drove to hospital. I got shaken and joggled the whole time, over an hour, but I kept playing dead. They laid me on a trolley, wheeled me in, pulled back my eyelids, took my pulse, undid my shirt, listened to my heart, slapped my cheeks and I still didnae stir.'

'Next thing I hear is a woman's voice in the corridor saying there was nothing to go on, all my vital signs were fine, I could be playacting. Another voice said not to take chances, to wire me up to a monitor. They would've had trouble with that since I was already halfway through the window.'

Both were enjoying Jamie's story, Jamie telling and Alex listening.

'I dropped to the car park and jumped a wall into the grounds of Glasgow Uni. Students were swarming all over the place and I definitely wasnae one of them in my detention outfit. I might as well have been wearing a big sandwich board saying, *On the Run.*'

'I'd kept fifteen quid hidden in the ticket pocket of my jeans, enough to buy a jacket on Byres Road but I spotted a polis car, so I stuck to the alleyways. I waved a fiver at some students in Ashton Lane, trying to act as friendly as I could, asking if they fancied swapping shirts for it. They sped up to get past me. I tried again with a squad of workers on a building site. A brickie swings down from a scaffold. He couldnae believe his luck — a fiver and a denim shirt for a tatty old rag.' Jamie pointed to the plaster-stained shirt lying in the corner.

'I was pulling it on when a polis car came along the road. The workers saw me crouching behind a pile of bricks, so one of them passes me a hard hat and another gives me a shovel. Good, eh? I helped them mix sand and cement for a while. I would've stayed until finishing time, to fall in with the crowd and that, only they started to wind me up. What had I done, robbed a bank, snow-dropped the washing lines, murdered someone? I just laughed and said I was innocent. I sneaked away and walked next to a group of babbling kids who were making their way down to Hillhead subway station, talking over each other about something that had happened in school. It was good cover. I caught the subway to Ibrox and made it back here around six.'

'They'll be hunting you.'

'I know. I hid here for a couple of hours, but I needed to see my granny, to tell her not to worry, and I needed some grub. This is the best bit... she opens the door and I'm staring straight at two big polis towering at her back... I says, *Is Jamie in*? My granny doesnae hesitate, she doesnae even blink, she says, *He's not here right now, son, he's in a spot of bother. It's best if you don't call back for a while.* That's what you call an escape, eh?'

'No half. Is that what happened?'

'Aye, gen-up. I goes back after they left, telt her I'd be staying with Lorna until I find out what happens to McPeat, get myself a better lawyer and then I'll hand myself in. She gives me dog's abuse for even thinking of bringing trouble to Lorna's door. Says I only ever think of myself.'

'You cannae live in here forever.'

'If McPeat gets off with a few months or probation, I'll do what my granny wants, but if he gets a year or more, I'm off. Away from here for good.'

'Do you want a milk delivery in the morning?' Alex said, half-joking.

'Good idea. Stick a couple of pints in the hedge.'

Alex caught up with him over the next couple of weeks. He seemed to be doing alright, although it was a certainty that things would not end well. He'd been seeing Lorna in the evenings and said that she knew everything that had happened, his version of it anyway, how the polis had set him up. He got pally with her parents too, and even went to church with them on Sundays. He didn't seem to do anything in half measures. He walked the railway to Tradeston, went looking for a job and found one in the Co-op warehouse in Morrison Street. It was the break he needed, stacking shelves from eight to four, a perfect way to hide during the day, and because he was old enough to work he'd have no problem in getting a National Insurance number. He fell into the routine, travelling on the bus with the other workers. He seemed relaxed and began sneaking home to his own bed until the days leading to McPeat's court case, when an unmarked police car was parked in the street for hours at a time.

On the day of the trial, Alex was making his way home from school, walking fast to keep well ahead of Shona, avoiding her. She had knocked his confidence, and he didn't have the courage to face her.

Reaching Corkerhill he spotted McPeat coming off the train and scampering along the track to escape the ticket collector. Next, Jamie came bounding out of a tenement close, where he'd been hiding all day, overlooking the station and the bus stop, hoping that McPeat would show. 'Hoi, Cornelius,' he shouted.

Alex caught up as they were sharing a fancy handshake that they'd learned in the remand home.

'Did you get fined?' Jamie asked.

'Nup, naff-all fine. Naff-all nothing. Them charges didnae stick. That lawyer was brilliant. He got the case chucked out. They cannae touch me now. I showed them two tecs the fingers.'

'You're a jammy wee sod. You think there's a chance they'll drop my charges?'

'Aye, nae chance. They're a-coming for you,' McPeat said. 'I only got off cause you bolted. The lawyer blamed you. You can blame me. That's how it works.' He glanced up the road. 'I have to get going to see my old dear. Catch you later.' He swaggered away in that walk of his — on his toes, arms swaying.

'Fuck sake,' Jamie said. 'One minute things are beginning to look okay and the next they're shite. I'm gonni need escape money… are you still up for the mansion?'

'If you are.'

'I'll go suss it and let you know.'

Wine Alley Boys

Alex couldn't come up with the right thing to say to Shona, not the way he wanted to say it. At least he'd finally made up his mind, and was outside her house ready to ask her, straight out, why she was with Haw. But it was all bravado, because he lost his nerve when Missus Coghlin answered the door. He asked for Nathan instead.

That boy, she said, was hanging around somewhere knocking himself stupid with drink and dope and would probably fall in a hedge or a ditch and freeze to death in this weather. She asked Alex to find him and keep an eye on him.

She was right about the drink and dope. Nathan was on a settee in the field in front of a bonfire, puffing on a joint and supping from a can of Tennent's lager. He had a stack of them at his feet and his cassette recorder by his side, playing '*Gimme Shelter.*' A group of teenagers, boys and girls, were hanging around nearby with their own supply of booze.

Enjoying a fire in the crispy cold December air and listening to decent music seemed like a good idea. And knocking yourself stupid didn't seem too bad either.

Nathan pointed his joint at the moon. 'It's hard to imagine that spacemen were bouncing around up there a few weeks ago.'

Three quarters of the moon, as big and as clear and yellow as Alex had seen, had risen over the forest in the cloudless night sky. He lifted a can and stood facing the fire.

'Help yourself, why don't you?' Nathan said.

Alex answered by raising his hand. His mind was still on Shona, coming to a new decision — it was up to her to speak to him if she wanted.

The bonfire drew more people, and Jamie and McPeat showed up a while later. Both looked cold and miserable, McPeat limping.

Jamie picked up a can.

'Help yourself, why don't you?' Alex said, copying Nathan.

Nathan slackened the hood of his army parka. It had been covering his face. 'Aye, join the party. Next time bring your own.'

'Am I getting one?' McPeat asked.

'Go ahead. At least you've got manners.'

'What happened to your leg?'

'My ma's boyfriend. That bastard. That's what happened. Scudded me on the shin with a poker, so he did. Blamed me for the polis coming to the hoose. I'm gonni be staying in Jamie's den from now on.'

Jamie punched him on the arm. 'I telt you to keep it to yourself, big mouth. You'd be as well standing at the top of the hill with a megaphone making a big hear-ye, hear-ye declaration.'

'Aye alright, Jamie. I didnae mean it.'

'I'm on the run, mate. I shouldnae be telling naebody about my hideout. Remember to keep it buttoned. You've no seen me. Right?'

'Who said that?' McPeat laughed. He downed the can in three, burped and chucked the empty on the fire. 'And I'll tell you something else about that bastard. It's him who's tanning the hooses, so it is. I've seen the piles of ten pences he steals from the gas and electric meters. He spends it at the bookies, so he does. He spends my ma's dole money an all. She's never got enough to pay for nowt. Them sheriff officers came and took the telly. They're gonni chuck her on the street if she doesnae cough up the rent.'

'Well, she isnae kipping in the howf with us,' Jamie joked.

'I'll no be able to play fitba for months. I was supposed to be getting signed, so I was. It's no fair.'

'Neither's a hair on King Kong's arse.'

'It's no funny neither.'

Nathan puffed on the joint. 'Get the violins, this is getting sadder by the minute.'

'Well, it's true. It's no easy being me. My ma says she's sorry for bringing me into this world. And how come Jamie didnae tell me about his den when I'm in the Hillman Imp for two nights, freezing to death?'

No one replied.

'I wish the whole world was like playing fitba.'

Jamie shook his head. 'Try getting to sleep with him near you. I'm edgy myself, but no half as bad as he is. He fights in his sleep and takes a hairy fit whenever he hears the birds shifting in the bushes. Nearly jumps out his skin at the baying foxes.'

'Where d'you eat?' Nathan asked.

'He's never got nowt for eating.'

'What d'you expect?' said Jamie, 'Ham and eggs?'

'My ma gives me custard creams for breakfast. Much better than the crap you get in the nick.'

Nathan handed McPeat another can. 'Don't you have cornflakes in your hoose?'

'Don't like them. My old dear buys them fake ones from Galbraith. No matter how much sugar you put on them, they still taste shite, and them wee hard bits nearly break your teeth.'

'Hannaaaah!'

The shout was Grogan's. He came through the haze of the fire, staggering towards them with a wine bottle in his hand, his fist tight around the neck of it.

Jamie stepped in close, giving him no room to swing it. 'It's yourself, Phil. C'mon give us a slug of the plonk and help yourself to a can.'

'Don't mention hogweed,' McPeat whispered.

Grogan stood there in his Crombie coat, half-closed eyes, daft with drink.

'Lanliq,' said Jamie, reading the label on the wine bottle. 'Electric soup.'

'Brock,' said Nathan.

'Jungle juice,' said McPeat. 'Vino collapso.'

Grogan stuck out his arm, offering the bottle to whoever wanted it.

Nathan took it, squinted down the neck and sniffed it before slugging on it. Alex, Jamie, and McPeat did likewise, each taking a swig and screwing their faces at the bittersweet burning taste.

Grogan hadn't spoken and was still giving them the mad-eye stare.

Jamie kept hold of the bottle and kept up his efforts to win him over. 'Remember that time we tried to raid that place in Tradeston? Must've been a hundred of us.'

'I'll never forget it,' Nathan said. 'Bunch of eejits got me the sack from my delivery-boy job. I hated losing that bike.'

'How many you had?' Grogan said.

'What? Cans?'

'Jobs. How many?'

Nathan, counting with his fingers, said, 'Six.'

'I cannae even find one.'

'Aye, six. Got sacked for poor timekeeping. Cannae blame them, I was hardly ever there.'

'What's the worse you've had?'

'Jobs?'

'Aye.'

'Let me think... a tea boy in Govan shipyard. That was the shittiest. The foreman was a right bastard. He threw a biscuit in my face because it had a green wrapper. Told me to go back to the shops and change it for a blue one. What a halfwit. I did what he wanted, but only after sticking an LSD tab in his corned beef chit. He left work early… said he was seeing things.'

Grogan sat next to Nathan on the couch. 'Want to know what happened to me the night? Some old guy in the pub was shouting at me, telling me that I knew fuck-all... that Johnstone was a better player than Baxter. I put the nut on him for that. I'll batter anybody who noises me up.'

A shiver of hate ran through Alex. Why were they even talking to this idiot? 'They wouldnae even let you in a pub,' he said.

'Shut it Hannah or you'll be getting malkied.'

'Here. You need the peace pipe, man,' Nathan said, offering Grogan the joint. 'A few draws on this gear and you'll be kissing people no fighting them.'

Grogan took it and puffed away. And it worked. He slumped back sat on the settee and his eyes glazed over even more than usual. 'I went for a gravedigger's job once,' he mumbled. 'The guy asked me to show my sad face. Said it wasnae sad enough, so I never got a start.'

The others couldn't stop laughing — pretty sure he was being serious.

On hearing *Maggie May* on the cassette recorder, Nathan turned up the volume and sang along. Everyone joined-in, including the boys and girls who were hanging around, belting it out at the top of their voices. Next came *Mandolin Wind,* getting the same backing vocals.

When the fire sunk to dying embers, they chucked the couch on top, and flames soon soared into the night sky, a sudden burst of heat and colour.

Jamie nudged Alex. 'Them crates are still there. I wiped the muck off the basement windows and peeked in with my torch. They're there alright, exactly like we remember. But they won't be for long. They're getting shifted to a new museum.'

'How d'you know?'

'It's in a newspaper I read at work. I'll bring it to you,' Jamie said, before getting off his mark at the sound of the wailing siren. The flames had been high enough for someone to call the fire brigade.

The next morning, rumours were flying around about the Wine Alley boys running riot with a shotgun. Someone had been shot and was lucky it was only a flesh wound. Alex got put straight when he met McPeat at the shop.

McPeat could hardly tell the story for laughing. He'd been in the howf in the dead of night when he heard footsteps on the Avenue. He slid open the spy-hatch and watched his mother's boyfriend sneaking up to the Hillman Imp and shaking it — the bastard probably thought McPeat was inside and was trying to frighten the life out of him. Jamie was awake by now. He lifted the air rifle from under the camp bed, loaded a pellet and rested it on the spy-hatch to let McPeat take over. McPeat lined up the sights and pulled the trigger. The bastard cried out, holding the back of his neck. Jamie took it, reloaded, aimed and fired, this time catching him on the arse. The two were creased up, struggling to stifle their giggles for the rest of the night.

'Shouldnae let that Wine Alley mob think they rule the place, but we'll forgive them this time,' McPeat joked, before loping off to watch his team playing.

That evening, a squad car pulled into the scheme. The boys on the corner split, heading along Corkerhill Road and some making for the back gardens. The car followed McPeat and Cammy Sinclair, crawling along beside them. 'You're no moving fast enough.'

McPeat only said, 'Big wow!' But it was enough for both boys to be collared on breach of the peace charges — *shouting and swearing and acting in a threatening manner*. Cammy got the social work treatment — home visits and reports. McPeat got six months. A short, sharp shock, they called it.

Alex did not see him again.

Clipping

Jamie wasn't one for coming to your door, but there he was, his clothes hanging off him, baggy, like they had grown too big.

'You look like death warmed-up. You want to come in for something to eat?'

'Nah.'

'A drink?'

'I'm fine.'

'So, you've no been nabbed yet.'

'No yet.'

'Huvnae seen you for a few days. Thought you might've been nabbed.'

'No yet.'

'You're getting skinnier.'

Jamie slid a newspaper clipping from his back pocket. 'You're getting like my granny. Give us a break and have a look at this.'

Alex took it and walked to the stair light, unfolded it and read it.

"The scandal of the famous Burrell Collection languishing in dusty storerooms is about to end. Glasgow Corporation has selected the winner of a competition to design a bespoke museum. The new building will be an elegant, modern solution, exploiting the natural surroundings of old Pollok Estate, finally allowing the people of Glasgow to see and admire the ancient artefacts."

'We have to do it the night. It's all arranged. I went in with the tourists and had a right good look at them upstairs windows. They don't have bars like the ground floor. They've got wooden shutters with a steel locking plate and an alarm that sounds if the contacts get broken. The main doors are wired too, so—'

'So there's nae chance.'

'Has your old buddy no gone and found an easy way in? Of course I have, or I wouldnae be here telling you this. Listen, there's two sets of shutters on some windows but the alarm only covers the bottom ones. That's the weak spot. I hid until the last of the tourists were leaving. Waited till I heard the caretaker shuttering-up... the clanging and that. Waited till I heard him on the far side of the hall, then made my move. I undid a locking plate and balanced it so it's ready to fall at the slightest push. I was outside long before he'd finished. We only need to jemmy the sash window and we're in! The place is dubbed-up for Christmas now. It's perfect. There shouldnae be anybody around.'

'Shouldnae be doesnae mean there isnae.'

Jamie paced back and forth. 'I've got a good feeling about it, mate, it'll be more dosh than we can handle.'

'Keep still, will you?'

'Cannae help it. I'm raring to go. It'll be a shoo-in.'

'Who'll buy the stuff?'

'Melville.'

'But he'll rip us off.'

'We won't let him.'

'How?'

'He'll be slobbering over all that ancient gear. We'll tell him about it, but we only give him one piece at a time, see? That way he won't have the chance to con us. He has to give us a good deal or we go elsewhere with the rest of the gear.'

'How much d'you plan on taking?'

'Two duffel bags worth. We'll settle for nothing less than fifty-fifty on the deal. Melville's gonni bite our hands off for it. I'm sure.'

'You sure they're worth what we think they're worth?'

'Dead sure.'

'You cannae hide from the polis forever.'

'I was gonni go live at my granny's sister's in Inverness. Get a job in the oilrig yards. Then my own digs. Lorna said she'd come and stay with me. I asked my granny to sort it, but she says she'd never bother her sister with my troubles. I argued with her, said I'd top myself if I got locked in the nick. I stormed out.'

'You shouldnae have said that.'

'Look, I didnae mean it. I've got too much on my mind. I'll go back and tell her I'm sorry.'

Jamie took the newspaper clipping and tore it up. 'I've got it all worked out.' He stared straight at Alex. 'You up for it, aye or naw?'

'I'm thinking about it.'

'The clock's ticking. You gonni wind up skint like all the big-talkers roundabout here who never do nowt except spend their crap wages in the pubs and bookies, eh? C'mon, mate, what do you say? It'll be much easier with the two of us. It's what you've always talked about.'

The daring in Alex told him that the Burrell antiques were just waiting to be nicked. They deserved to be. Fair's fair. He knew every inch of the park and knew there was plenty of time to sneak out of the house, get to the mansion, get inside, jemmy the packing crates, fill a few bags, snatch the *Lady in the Fur Wrap*, hide it, and be home before anyone woke. The thrill of stealing that painting beat the worry of being caught.

He did not sleep that night. He waited until the luminous dial of his watch showed twenty-five past one. His clothes were in a neat bundle at his bedside and the house was sound asleep. He dressed quietly, took two strides across the hall and opened the door quickly so that it didn't squeak. He left it off the latch and made his way downstairs to meet Jamie.

They spoke in whispers.

'You ready?'

'Ready.'

'Anybody spot you?'

'Don't think so.'

Jamie held up a duffel bag. 'Take it. There's gloves, a tammy and a torch inside. Keep the torch off till we get there.'

Nae Scary Men

They treaded soundlessly on the soft damp grass, snuck past the sleeping bedrooms and did not speak again until they had left the streets and were crossing the golf course. A breeze was getting up, adding to the cold night air.

'A storm's coming,' Alex said.

'How's that?'

'My ma says so. The washing was blowing the wrong way on the balcony.'

'Oh well, it must be true.'

With only enough light to make out the metal bar fence at the farmer's field, they stuck to it, walking most of its length before climbing to cross to the woods. Wetter underfoot, they were struggling through sucking mud when the sound of heavy shuffling sent them retreating in a panic, plodding and slipping their way to the fence, tumbling over it. As they stared back into the darkness, the moon shone through a break in the clouds revealing a fold of Highland cows, huddling together and backing off as if they were the ones who were frightened.

'Freaking heart attack!'

Jamie wiped the soles of his boots on the fence. 'I knew it was coos.'

'Aye, sure you did.'

'What are they hairy beasts doing out here at this time of night? Should they no be in a barn?'

'Do I look like a farmer?'

'See that one. The one at the front, it's pure raging, like it's ready to charge.'

The cow at the front let go a loud splashing pee and the boys fell into a giggling fit, hands on each other's shoulders.

Once inside the forest their nerves were tested again. They could see only shadows, different shades of shadow, black ones against deep bluish ones, and fallen leaves twitched as if something was following them. They walked on slowly, hands out for trees and God-knows-what. Without saying a word they moved steadily closer to each other, shoulder touching shoulder, instinct telling them to veer to the outside edge, open space to their left in case they had to make a run for it.

The tingling in Alex's belly worsened at the sight of the mansion. The place seemed part of the darkness, never ending.

'Follow me,' Jamie said, jumping the garden wall.

They crept round the building. A downpipe was spilling water onto the pebbles in the courtyard. The sound of it took the edge off Alex's nerves, but not for long. Seeing a parked car, he nudged Jamie and pointed. 'There could be someone in there watching us.'

'There's naebody.'

'There might be.'

Jamie walked up and pressed his nose to the windscreen.

'See? Nae scary men.'

'I'm shaking.'

'It's adrenaline, mate. You get used to it.'

Alex kept the other doubts to himself, including that shadow at an upstairs window. Maybe it was somebody who had called the polis.

Two ledges within easy reach helped the climb. From the bottom one and holding on to the top one, Jamie pressed himself flat against the wall and shimmied along to a first-floor window. He dragged himself up to the sill, slid the duffel bag from his shoulder, removed the jemmy and kissed it. 'Do your stuff,' he said. He levered it against the top corner of the window, jerking down the sash panel by five or six squeaky inches, then stuck his hand through the gap and pushed on the shutters. The locking plate fell away inside, clattering. An almighty echoing racket. He held up a hand as a signal to stay put.

Set and ready to scamper at the faintest sign of life, Alex did not move an inch.

'There cannae be anybody for miles. You'd have heard that in Timbuktu, so you would,' Jamie said in a hissing whisper, like he wasn't sure. He waited another minute or two before forcing his weight on the window. This time it gave out a long squeak. 'It's paint-stuck... but wide enough.'

He disappeared in one slick move.

Getting to the sill and through the open window was easy, but Alex struggled to upright himself on the inside.

Jamie shone his torch. 'Grab the corners. Lift a leg. Now the other one. Clamp your bum cheeks on the edge. The old bum-clamp comes in handy now and again!'

Alex's feet found the top of a radiator. 'Very funny,'

'It's too late to turn back nooooooow,' Jamie said, holding the torch under his chin.

Another round of nervous laughing was brought to a stop as the floorboards creaked under their weight.

'Watch!' Jamie said, pointing his torch at the floor.

'Eh?'

'There could be pressure pads.'

'What?'

'Alarms.'

'What alarms?'

'Keep off the pads.'

'What pads?'

'Just watch where you put your big feet.'

'Now you tell me.'

They creaked through the rooms. On reaching the library, Alex guided his torch over the walls and found the painting.

'Forget it mate. Stick with the plan.'

'I'm taking it.'

'You cannae. It's wired. Bugged with silent alarms that'll set bells ringing at the polis station.'

Planning to snatch it on the way out, Alex moved on behind Jamie.

The double doors on the upper landing clicked open, leading to the staircase and down to the iron gate in the basement. It rattled and scraped as they dragged it along its runners, the noise echoing up a small turnpike staircase in the corner, even louder than the window racket. Reflexes caused them to switch off their torches.

After another few moments of not moving, Alex shone his torch along the corridor. The beam of light was too weak to reach the far end, making the place seem foggy, even creepier than it was. 'C'mon, Jamie. We've hung around too long,' he said. The jitters kept him talking. He introduced each of the doors, a bit like Mister Mackenzie had done. 'The butler's pad, Jeeves's pad, the kitchen, the coal bunker—'

'And this is where the goodies live,' Jamie said, stepping up to the last door and trying the handle.

It wouldn't budge.

'It's snecked.'

'Now what?'

Sounding confident, Jamie took a bunch of keys from his bag. 'Some people... they've just got nae consideration for others.'

The barrel of the first key wouldn't fit, the second one refused to turn, the one after that turning only halfway.

'Hurry, we huvnae got all night.'

'Keep the faith, mate.'

After five or six attempts, a key slid in, clicked twice, and the door yawned open as if it was in a Dracula movie.

They swished their torches over the packing crates. The lid of the nearest one was propped at the side, loose straw lying around it. Jamie dug in, groped around and lifted out something with both hands. He held it to his chest and stripped away layers of paper, uncovering a white stone bust of some ancient guy with a crown of flowers. A label dangled from it.

'It's been accounted for. See if you can find stuff with nae labels.'

'Too heavy anyhow.' Jamie said. He put it back in its place, climbed over the crates and jemmied off two lids, side by side. 'You do that one, I'll do this.'

He had hold of a vase by the time Alex scrambled up next to him. 'Look, nae label.'

Alex scarched beneath the straw for a few seconds before he touched something. It felt like a metal cup. He fished it out and aimed his torch at it. Tiny rainbows shone through the red and green glass on the rim. No label.

They plucked unlabelled objects of all shapes and sizes from those two crates, stuffing the duffel bags until there was room for no more, then used the jemmy to knock the lids back on and used their feet to sweep the spilt straw underneath.

To lock the storeroom behind them, Jamie had to search for the right key all over again.

'You should've left it in the door, daftie. You're supposed to be good at this.'

Closing the iron gate, it scraped and grated once again. No point in stopping now. They bounded up the stairs, the antiques chinking inside the bags as they went.

Jamie climbed out first, onto the sill, and stuck his hands back into the room. 'Quick. Pass them through.'

But the bags were too big and bulky for the gap. Alex was forced to remove a few of the bigger pieces, hand them to Jamie and wait for him to carry them to the ground one at a time, until both bags were skinny enough. Alone in the mansion, it seemed the room was closing in. He rushed to drag himself up and out, lost balance on the sill, jumped onto the grass, rolled and hit one of the bags. Something jingled. Whatever it was, it was smashed to pieces.

'That's coming out of your wages,' Jamie joked as he climbed back up to the window. He pulled the shutters over, then heaved his shoulder against the sash panel trying to close it. He couldn't.

'You need to get up here and help.'

'Forget it. We need to go.'

To stop the bags from tinkling and to avoid damaging any more of the antiques, they walked fast instead of running, stretching strides along the edge of the forest at pace. The wind, beginning to bite, was making branches creak and groan above their heads. Only now did Alex realise that, in his panic to get out, he had left the painting behind.

It was nearing half-four when they reached the railway. The whirring of the diesel engines meant that the nightshift was in full swing. They dropped silently to the turntable pit and crawled into the space under the track. They were stashing the bags among the girders when the lines twanged. The turntable rattled and dust showered them as a train thundered up the main line. It echoed on and on into the night.

The glow of cigarettes stopped them from climbing out. Two railway workers were at the dump, smoking and talking in murmurs.

'We'll freeze to death if they don't get a move on,' Alex said.

'Skiving bastards.'

The railway men finally moved on, and the boys bolted, relieved they were no longer carrying the stolen goods. At least they couldn't be caught red-handed. Before splitting up the avenue, they agreed to meet at one in the afternoon.

Alex was sure that he hadn't been spotted, except by Homeless. The big mutt came bounding up to him, sniffing and whining for its food.

He spoke to it softly. 'Shush boy. Shush. I'll be down later.' He stroked it, and it gave out a low growl as if it understood.

At the top of the stairs he took deep breaths to compose himself, opened the door and latched it behind him and went into the bathroom and slowly washed his hands, face and neck.

In bed by five o'clock, he hoped for an hour's sleep before getting up for the milk round. The next thing was the stink of smelly socks dangling in his face.

Forbes was the joker. 'You've slept in by miles. Da tried to wake you but you just grunted.'

Alex swung his legs over the side of the bed and sat there, taking a moment to come round. He squinted at his watch. It was gone twelve.

He got up to a stack of comments from his parents.

'Too many early mornings catching up with you.'

'You need your sleep.'

'You must feel better for it.'

'You should think about packing in that milk round.'

Kings and Queens

Broken clouds raced over the spaces in the track above their heads as they sat below the turntable facing each other with big stretchy toothy grins that just couldn't be helped, the duffel bags by their side.

'You first,' said Jamie.

Alex delved-in and took care to remove a Chinese vase, then another, passing them to Jamie. One was white and blue with hexagon patterns and one yellow with motifs of blue fish and brown leaves. Next out was a dumpy metal flask carved like an owl. Alex, not sure what he was looking for, turned it over in his hands, inspecting it. Jamie did too, before setting it down alongside the vases. The metal cup was next, followed by its twin, both decorated with rings of coloured stones.

'Rubies and sapphires. We're minted. We're gonni need deeper pockets for all the cash.'

'Don't get too carried away. It's probably glass,' Alex said.

'Stop being a... what do you call them people who're always seeing the worse side of things?'

'Don't know.'

'Aye, well, stop being one.'

They stuck to the job of checking the antiques one by one until the first bag was empty. With half of the haul in front of them they were looking at two vases, an owl-shaped flask, the twin gemstone cups, a bronze Buddha about the size of a melon, a clay dog with a pig's tail, a winged horse and rider made from dull grey metal and the smashed to pieces vase.

Out of Jamie's bag came another two vases, not too different from the first two. Then a panther's head, carved in black marble. He seemed not to think much of it before passing it to Alex, who decided it was a lion, not a panther.

'Nowt, compared to this!' Jamie said, holding up a Madonna and Child statuette. 'I mean, if this is real? Real gold, eh? How much weight's in it?'

Alex took it, balanced it on his hand and closed his eyes.

'About the same as a bag of sugar.'

'A big bag or a wee bag?'

'A big bag. Two pounds.'

'That's sixteen ounces times two, about twenty quid an ounce. How much is that?'

'Six hundred and forty.'

'Split two ways if we get it melted.'

'It's more like brass to me, too dull for gold. And check the state of it. I mean, it's the gawkiest Madonna I've ever seen.'

Jamie laughed. 'Aye. You've got a point, mate. And clock baby Jesus, he looks older than my granny.'

The second last antique out of the duffel bags was a brass triple-headed dragon candlestick holder, and the final one was a stone bear, kneeling on a hind leg and holding up both of its front paws as if begging, its mouth open, showing big chunky square teeth with lots of gaps.

'Jade stone. I smell even more dosh.'

'We better remember it all,' Alex said. 'I'll mind the vases and the owl, the metal jugs and the wee baldy guy with the belly.'

'Right you are. I'll mind the flying horse, the pig-dog, the black lion and the bear with the gnashers and the candlestick thingy.'

'And the blessed Madonna. Better not forget her,' Alex said. He put on a newsreader's voice. 'Taken from under the very noses of the security guards.'

They sat there for a while, not yet ready to put the antiques back inside the bags.

'We done it,' Jamie said. 'Feels like scoring a hat-trick at Hampden.'

'More like Robin Hood. Here's us, we've gone and tanned the Sheriff. Stuff that's thousands and thousands of years old, stuff that ancient kings and queens once owned.'

'You're romancing again, mate.'

'It's pure history.'

'It's pure dosh. And we could've taken more of it.'

'Ah well, got to leave them something, I suppose.'

'Aye, cannae be too greedy.'

'Jamie.'

'That's me.'

'I was gonni take it.'

'Take what?'

'The painting. I forgot all about it in the rush to get away. Will you go back with me?'

'Am I fuck going back! You better be joking or you're off your rocker. The polis will be all over that place, hiding in the bushes with binoculars. Stay well clear.'

'You lied about it.'

'Eh?'

'I was with Nathan when he took it off the wall. There wasnae any alarm.'

'How do you know? It could've been wired-up since then.'

Alex didn't reply.

'Look, mate. I like the thought of it, but we cannae be too careful. It's far too risky. And the caretaker... he'll know something's up as soon as he sees the open window.'

'Maybe he'll say nothing if he thinks nothing's missing, or he'll get the boot for not locking-up properly.'

'I wouldnae bet on it. It's far too risky.'

'I heard you the first time.'

'You need to think differently from now on. Keep yourself safe.'

'How long till we start shifting it?'

'The pawn won't open until after the New Year. I'll take the flying horse first. Melville's gonni go ga-ga over it.'

They climbed up on the track and peered through the spaces in the sleepers, making sure that the bags couldn't be seen from above. Even in daylight it was too shadowy underneath. The stash would be safe.

Ghost or Something

If the antiques sold for thousands, imagine having all that money. Alex just needed a way to avoid suspicion. Maybe he could post wads of notes to his father, a gift from some distant relative. Then again, the antiques might not sell because they were too hot or maybe not worth more than a few quid. The scary problem — what would happen if he got caught? Strangely enough, there hadn't been a peep about it on the news, nothing in the papers, no stories on the streets and no polis hanging around asking questions. Taking the painting would've been different, definitely front-page stuff, like the Mona Lisa.

Should've taken it.

That thought grew in his head, especially after his mother had sunk back into herself at Christmas. It started well. She had been fine in the morning and had even surprised everyone with gifts she ordered from the mail-order catalogue, Old Spice for Da, half-decent shirts for the boys and a bundle of toys for Sarah. She switched on the wireless that Alex and Forbes had bought her, and she joked that Da wouldn't have to beat it up it to get a reception like the old one. By the afternoon though, she'd had enough — the happy ending film and the soppy reminiscing on telly. Too many painful reminders that stole her away. She went all quiet, gave up eating the turkey dinner, slipped off to bed and stayed there until the new year celebrations were over.

When school started back, Alex's job was to check out the museums while Jamie got a move on at the pawn. He browsed past thousands of objects in the McLellan Galleries on Sauchiehall Street, the Hunterian in the West End and the nearby Kelvingrove Art Gallery. He found nothing that matched the stuff in the duffel bags, although he did spot a statuette that came close to resembling the Wee China. He pointed too closely, asking how much it might be worth. The guard replied by warning him not to touch the artefacts or he'd be asked to leave. He left anyway, no wiser.

Miss Cleghorn did not ask for an excuse when he showed up in registration after being absent and missing the first of the mid-term exams, physics. She set a homework sheet on his desk and talked to the class in her usual upbeat way, not saying a word to him. Was she making a point? If he didn't care, then who would? He decided to be there for the remaining exams.

Desperate to know how the pawning business was going, he set out to find Jamie straight after school.

Shona came scurrying up behind him as he reached Hardridge.

'It's yourself, Alex.'

'Unless it's somebody that looks like me.'

She pulled down the hood of her duffel coat, shook her blonde hair and walked alongside.

'What are you gawking at?' he said.

'Don't know, the label's fell off.'

He blocked her out by booting an empty can along the pavement. The wind caught it and swirled it in the air.

'It's nice to be nice, you should try it,' she said.

She kept talking. He kept kicking the can.

'Me and Rita have been going to an over-eighteen disco called Clouds. Everyone goes there now.'

'Is that right?'

'You'd like it.'

He wanted to ask if she was seeing Haw but didn't want to show his feelings.

At the stairs to her house she realised he wasn't going home. 'Where are you off to?'

'Nowhere for nosey folk.'

'Are you alright?'

'Why wouldn't I be?'

'You're being all sneaky these days. I'll walk with you. I need to get something from the shop anyhow.'

'Suit yourself. I'm off to see Jamie,' he said, knowing she hated him.

'I warned you, sure I did? There're rumours about him and Lorna running away. But that won't happen because he'll be in the jail.'

'Listen to you gossiping. You'll be knitting jumpers soon, sitting in the porch like Missus Little, shaking a mop at the weans.'

She was about to reply when Jamie whistled from his window and waved frantically to attract their attention. 'Come up here,' he bawled. 'Both of you.'

'What d'you suppose he wants?' she said, shrugging.

'Let's go see.'

He met them at the door. 'You've to go through to the bedroom and see my granny.'

They were curious and stepped inside. At once the smell hit them and they saw her on the bed, mouth open, sunken eyes, ashen skin drawn tight on her dead skull.

Shona spun round and pulled the door handle. 'Open it!' she screamed.

'Stop making a racket, you'll waken her,' Jamie said from the hall. He was holding the door shut.

'Open it, Jamie, it's no funny. Your granny doesnae look good,' Alex said.

'Doesnae look good? Of course she doesnae fuckin look good. She's dead for Christsake!'

Jamie let go the handle, causing Shona to stumble and fall. She scrambled to her feet, slapped him hard across the cheek and ran.

'See a ghost or something?' he shouted after her.

Alex noticed the things on the bedside table, a bible, an alarm clock and a photo of a man in army uniform, things that were important to the old woman.

Jamie's laughing had turned to crying. The sobs came hard, jolting him as he spoke. 'She felt tired and went to lie down and stayed there and wouldnae eat. She only took wee totty sips of water. I called the doctor, and he checked her over and left medicine. But she wouldnae take it. Her breathing got smaller and smaller. And that was it. She just packed in.' He slumped on the floor, blinking tears.

Alex tried to think of words. He couldn't. He left to get help.

When he returned with Da, Jamie was still sobbing.

Da put his arm around Jamie's shoulders. 'That's it son, let it out. Let it all out.'

Beer Barrel

It was Da's suggestion that Jamie should sleep in the spare room until after the funeral. He needed looking-after, so long as he swore not to leave the house.

Sitting on the makeshift bed, he looked shattered. It wasn't right to be pestering him over the antiques, but Alex needed to know.

'I didnae even get to the pawn, mate,' he explained. 'Hardly had time to think about it, y'know.'

'Aye, I know. Sorry.'

'There's this thing I'm trying to get straight in my head. At the remand home, they said that if you get into deep enough trouble, then even your family will give up on you. There's only so much they'll put up with. Do you think that's true, mate? Did she give up on me?'

'That's rubbish, Jamie. Family never give up.'

'I cannae imagine her not being here.'

'It'll get better. You can stay here as long as you need. My old man's okay with that. Naebody needs to know.'

But someone knew, because the polis came at half five in the morning. Alex was grabbing a slice of toast, getting ready for his milk round, when he saw their cars pulling up — two plain-clothed detectives in a gleaming dark-blue Jaguar and two uniformed men in a squad car. He rushed to the spare room and shook Jamie awake, then Da.

Jamie didn't have time to get dressed. Standing by in his underpants and T-shirt, he waited until he heard the rap on the door, then climbed out the window, stretched for the downpipe and was up on the roof and gone.

Da told the polis that they'd been lied to. They were welcome to come in and see for themselves. They did. They peeked in every room. By then, the window had been closed, the bed covers stuffed in the cupboard.

The howf was empty when Alex checked later that morning. It was empty again that night and the following day. No sign of anyone having slept there. Thinking that Jamie might have scampered with the antiques, he went to the turntable pit, sneaked past the railway men, got to the space below the track and reached among the girders. He relaxed as he felt the lumpy shapes of the duffel bags.

There was no Jamie the next day or the next. He didn't even make an appearance at the church service.

The minister starting and ending the sermon by telling everyone that they had gathered to celebrate the life of a well-respected member of their community, Mabel Bryce, who had led a long and fulfilling Christian life, raising her son and her grandson in the faith, attending service every Sunday. It was her time to be saved, he added, which sounded weird to Alex.

Six men paired up, side by side, to carry the coffin on their shoulders. The mourners shuffled in behind, walking slowly along the aisle, mostly elderly men and women in black clothes.

Outside in the drizzling rain, people huddled in groups sheltering under umbrellas, and walked in turn to a white-haired woman. Hands clasped, 'Sad loss. Sad loss,' they said.

Mister Coghlin stood by her side and waved Alex over.

'This is Jamie's great aunt Morag.'

She spoke with a Highland accent. 'Can you please ask Jamie to come and talk to me? I'll be at his house later this evening. Will you please do that for me?'

'But I don't know where he is.'

'Have you no idea?'

Alex shook his head.

'None at all?'

'Sorry. I'll tell him if I see him.'

She got into a limousine with the minister. It was followed by a procession of cars as it moved slowly behind the hearse.

Alex, Forbes and Da walked the short distance to the graveyard along with Shona, her parents and a few other neighbours. Ma couldn't cope with a funeral. She stayed at home with Sarah.

The coffin was laid on batons across the open grave. Cords, one end tied to the shiny brass handles, were passed to the men, and used to raise it, so that the batons could be slid from underneath. At that point, Jamie elbowed his way through the crowd, Lorna holding on to him. He took a cord and helped lower his grandmother to the earth.

After the cords were dropped, rattling on the coffin lid like a drum roll, the minister said the last prayer. Morag then ushered Jamie and Lorna to the limousine and sorted everyone into cars for the trip to the Crookston Hotel.

The Hannahs, the Coghlins, the Sinclairs and Missus Little sat together at one of the circular tables in the lounge. A waitress served from a tray, whisky or sherry for the adults and orange juice for anyone who wanted it.

'It was a nice service.'

'It was, aye.'

'In her eighties.'

'A good innings.'

'A good innings right enough.'

'That minister. He's good at funerals. Always finds the right things to say.'

'Always makes a point of getting to know you once you're a goner,' Mister Coghlin said.

'It's always wet and windy at that graveyard.'

'What'll that boy do with himself now? Not yet sixteen and in a heap of trouble.'

'That was a nasty thing he did to my Shona. I mean, locking her in the room with a dead body and all. She's been getting nightmares, sure you have, Shona?'

'Oh, Mammy. It wasnae that bad.'

Next came bowls of soup and sandwiches. And after an hour or so of small talk, people began making their way outside. Jamie, Lorna and Morag stood at the exit, thanking them for coming. Jamie, doing his knuckle cracking thing and shuffling nervously from foot to foot, spoke to Alex. 'Talk later, mate. Meet you the night in the howf.'

But he didn't make it to the howf. He didn't even make it out of the car park. The two plain-clothed detectives sprang from behind a stack of beer barrels, rugby-tackled him, twisted his arms up his back, forced his face to the gravel and handcuffed him. Lorna screamed as they dragged him to the Jaguar.

Mister Coghlin pleaded with them, placing his hand on the arm of one of the detectives. 'Go easy. He's just buried his grandmother this morning.'

'I'll fuckin bury you if you don't mind your own fuckin business,' the detective said through his teeth. He kicked Mister Coghlin in the groin sending him to the ground.

Now Shona and Missus Coghlin were screaming. People began jostling the polis, brollies and handbags swinging.

Glass smashed.

Silence.

Loud hissing.

Forbes had hurled a beer barrel through the front windscreen of their car, and beer was spraying up in a fountain of froth.

'Jesus Christ! Get him away from here,' Da said.

Alex grabbed hold of his brother and they left by the main road, hurried down to the banks of the river and followed it through Pollok to the pine forest at Corkerhill farm.

'I'm for it. They'll be up at our door,' Forbes said, leaning on the fence and staring at the cows in the field.

Alex was inside the woods out of the rain. 'Don't worry about it, Forbes. Naebody saw you amongst all that rammy. I didnae even see you. You'll be fine. The polis deserved it anyway, sure they did?'

Forbes yanked a handful of dock leaves and offered them to the nearest cow. It ambled up to him, took them and munched them, grating its jaws sideways. 'They love dock leaves, it gets them drunk,' he said.

'Never.'

'Aye, it makes them stagger.'

'A drunk coo?'

'I've even seen a coo greeting once. No bawling or nothing, just big tears running down its face.'

'First a drunk coo, then a greeting coo. You're having me on.'

Forbes came into the woods and sat on a low branch. His twitch had come back.

'Imagine them trying to explain it to their bosses,' Alex said. 'Brand-new Jag, smashed-in windscreen, beer barrel in the front seat and a puddle of pale ale on the floor. It'll be stinking for weeks.'

Forbes gave no reply. Not even a smile.

'It's me that's worried anyhow,' Alex said.

'How? What did you do?'

'Listen. If I tell you a big secret, the biggest you've ever heard... I mean really big, d'you promise you won't say a word?'

'You know I won't.'

After what had happened, Alex wanted to share his own troubles. It could make them both feel better. He ended up telling Forbes everything about the break-in — what it felt like to be so wound up that you could hardly speak, the forest at night, the silence, the screeching of the iron gate that sent shivers through you, the foggy basement, the antiques in the duffel bags, and almost getting stuck in the turntable pit because of the railway workers.

'Is it true? When?'

'Remember the morning I slept in?'

'I thought that was odd, you never sleep in.'

'I'll need to move the stuff now that Jamie's been nabbed.'

'Don't! You'll end up in the clink an all. Don't go near it.'

'I cannae be sure what's for the best. I could just leave them there for Jamie. They won't lock him up forever. Or maybe I should hide them in a better place.'

'What do you think Ma and Da would do if any of us got put away?'

'I know.'

'Then leave them be.'

Tizzy

Down-and-outs packed the back rows of the public gallery. They had come in out of the January cold. Alex and his father sat next to Morag and Lorna at the front, alongside the whispering families of the offenders.

'Breach of the Peace' charges from the weekend football matches took up most of the morning, slow and boring, apart from the entertainment of the down-and-outs who coughed and sniggered as the police officers read out accounts of their arrests. Funny how the accused had supposedly been shouting and swearing in a posh voice.

Just before twelve o'clock, the wigged sheriff announced that there was time for one more case before lunch. Jamie was led in, looking ruffled and tired, and the side of his face was scabbed-up from being dragged across the gravel. He waved at Lorna then watched the floor as the procurator read out the charges — absconding from custody and possession of stolen goods from Her Royal Majesty's Post Office, twenty-four pounds worth of saving stamps.

At least it was only two charges. Not so bad. The defence lawyer must have done his job. He got his turn to speak after Jamie pleaded guilty.

'James Bryce is a young teenager, a child under the law, who is full of remorse. He has owned-up to his crimes and will accept his punishment. I do wish to point out, my Lord, that in relation to the absconding offence, he fled, not from the remand home, but from a hospital where he was recovering after being beaten-up while in custody. He fled to be by the side of his sole guardian, his grandmother, in the last few days of her life. He is aware that this is not an excuse, my Lord. Nevertheless, I would request that you take it into account. I would also draw notice to the reference letter from his relative, Morag Cummings.'

The sheriff sifted through his papers, read them for a while and then looked down over his glasses at Jamie. 'Do you wish to say anything?'

'Only what the lawyer said, sir.'

The sentences that morning had ranged from small fines to thirty days, so it was a bit of a shock when Jamie got fourteen months, especially to Lorna who gasped and sobbed. As if to explain himself, the Sheriff said it could have been much longer if not for the mitigating circumstances of the absconding charge.

As soon as they were outside the court building, Da said what Alex expected him to say, reminding him that he now had two buddies in the nick, two boys who were about to learn the hard way, adding that life wasn't a rehearsal. He had a point.

Jamie's sentence was frightening. Fourteen months for a few saving stamps.

With that fresh in his mind, Alex couldn't risk taking anything to the pawn. He went there only to hear what the pawnbroker had to say about the antiques, and maybe make a deal.

Melville Samuels acted as if he didn't recognise him. 'You got a ticket?'

'Me and my mate, we pawned an ornament a while back.'

'I get barrow-loads of ornaments in here.'

'A Chinese statuette that sold for five hundred at auction and you only got forty-five, remember?'

Melville rubbed his chin.

'I've got more things like it, lots more.'

'Where's your mate? What did you say his name was?'

'He's moved away.'

'In the nick, is he?'

'His family flitted.'

'These things, what are they?'

'There's four Chinese vases, there's carved stone animals, jade and marble, there's a Madonna that could be solid gold, metal cups with rubies, a flying horse and—'

'Who's looking for them, Aladdin?'

'Naebody's looking for them.'

'Where did you get them?'

'From Aladdin.'

'Listen son, you're entitled to pawn whatever you like. If the ticket expires, I'm entitled to get rid of it. Bring them in and

I'll appraise them. Give you an estimate. I seem to recall a statuette. A religious piece from memory.'

'The same as before, fifty-fifty?'

'Let's see the goods first.'

'What if I bring them one at a time and you sell them one at a time?'

'Seems sensible. The sooner the better.'

Although pleased at that exchange, Alex hadn't yet convinced himself of the next move, not helped by his lack of trust in Melville. After mulling things over that night, he made up his mind to let things be for now. He'd go back to school, sit the remaining exams, to lessen the trouble he was in for missing the first two, then decide.

The maths paper was torture. He couldn't concentrate and had to read the questions over and over to get the gist. Kept getting different answers when he checked. With three questions from ten still to attempt, he looked to the clock on the wall and noticed Lorna beckoning to him through the glass panel on the classroom door.

He said he was done and got permission to leave.

In the corridor, Lorna glanced right and left, clasping Alex's hand as she did so. 'We need talk about those things you stole from the mansion. Jamie could get years added on for that.'

He did not have to act surprised. He was. He'd taken a step back from her. 'What are you on about?'

'He tells me everything and I tell him everything. We don't have secrets. He says you've to get rid of them, chuck them in the river, stuff them in the middens, anywhere they won't be found.'

'Get rid of what?'

'Come off it... I'm begging you.' She stopped talking while a bunch of first-year girls passed, then her eyes closed for a moment. 'We've got better things to worry over.'

'Like?'

She pulled her shirt tight to her tummy. 'Can't you see my bump?'

It took a few seconds to grasp the obvious. He felt his cheeks flushing. 'What are you gonni do with a baby? I mean, how are you gonni—'

'I know what you mean, Alex. It's causing a right tizzy, up the duff at fifteen, eh? I've even got my own social worker.'

He knew nothing clever to say to that.

'Jamie needs a wee bit of help after all he's been through. He's a good person. My parents like him too. He'll be living with us when he gets out... until he finds a job and we can get a place of our own. But you have to ditch that stolen stuff. It could ruin everything for us.'

'Aye... well... to tell the truth, I've been thinking about getting shot of it anyhow. It's too much hassle. I was waiting to hear from Jamie.'

'I'm telling you what he wants.'

'Thought I'd have heard from him by now... could've sent me a visitor's pass.'

'It's hard for him. He'll send you one once he settles. Will you do us this favour? Please. It's best for you too.'

'Aye. I'll do it.'

'Oh that's great! Will you tell me when it's done?'

'I won't hang around. I'll do it the night.'

It was dark when he got home from school. He made up a slice of bread and jam, took a swig of milk and left for the turntable, saying he wouldn't be gone long. He planned to move the bags to a safer place, bury them and leave them be until he talked to Jamie.

But they were gone.

They were meant to be tucked between the girders next to the wheels. His hands moved over every inch of the cold steel and found nothing. He looked around the pit. Nothing. He dashed back to the street and looked in the howf and took the keys and a torch and opened Jamie's cellar. Nothing. Then back to the turntable, searching with the torch. Nothing. Non-stop thoughts raced through his mind. Did a railway worker find them? Hadn't they checked they were well hidden? Did they check well enough? He was sure they did, so it must have been Jamie. He must have moved them before the funeral. Aye, that made sense. Jamie had moved them and hadn't told Lorna, and she was acting on her own, trying to fix things for her boyfriend. Alex wanted to believe that, but other possibilities crossed his mind. What if Da had found out? It wasn't hard to imagine him taking them straight back to the mansion and leaving them on the doorstep like an abandoned baby. Or maybe Forbes blabbed to someone who blabbed to someone who went and nicked them? You couldn't exactly go complaining to the polis that your knocked off treasures had been knocked off.

He was no clearer after talking to Forbes, because Forbes swore, cross-his-heart, that he hadn't told a soul.

To see Lorna's reaction was the only reason he went to school in the morning.

She was waiting for him at the gates. 'Well?'

'Well what?'

She sighed and gave him a nudge. 'Well, did you do it?'

'You've no need to worry now.'

'What happened?'

'I smashed them into wee tiny pieces and scattered them all over the dump. I'm glad to be rid of them,' he said, watching her closely. Her eyes told him she was genuinely relieved at what she thought was the truth. This gorgeous girl. What had Jamie done to deserve a girlfriend like her?

She hugged him and kissed him on the cheek. 'Oh Alex. You don't know what this means to me.'

'Nae bother. Tell Jamie to send me a visitor's pass, will you?'

'I will. But don't go writing. That's the worst thing. They open all the letters in that place.'

Turnpike

February brought rain, gales and sleet. It did not stop Alex from combing as much of the park as he could, hunting for signs of digging in the woods, around the sycamore stump and along the riverbank. He crossed the arched bridge to Pollok golf course and sat on his heels on top of the mound of the ancient burial ground. No way Jamie would've hidden the antiques in there.

Trying not to act suspiciously became more and more difficult, thinking that people were watching his every move — golfers, green keepers, railway men, dog walkers, maybe even plain-clothed detectives. He cut down on his search. Talking to Jamie, eye to eye, was the only way. Lorna swore that she had asked him to arrange a visitor's pass, but since he was being moved to borstal, it could take a while.

By April he still hadn't heard from Jamie, and Lorna was off school with the pregnancy business. It crossed his mind more than once that he'd been conned out of the antiques. No doubt Jamie had tricked him out of taking the painting. Having the chance and not taking it now felt like a bigger let down than losing the antiques.

He hadn't planned anything, he just got up for his milk round two hours earlier than usual, 3:45, pulled on his clothes, gloves and hat, left the door off the latch, same as before, and stepped outside. The voice in his head told him he was kidding himself to think the painting could help anything. He didn't care.

Taking a different route this time, he stuck to the open ground and followed the line of moonlit treetops alongside the river. Out there alone, the wind played tricks on his mind. He kept hearing noises, and after a while convinced himself that children were playing in the woods. He could hear them chanting. It brought on a sense of the night terrors. The same terrors he'd had in hospital — hearing and eyesight charged as if by electricity, intense fear, time racing past. There was no way of telling how long he stood in the cold air before realising he was listening to the splashing of the waterfall. He moved on, shivering.

'Get a grip.'

'There's no such thing as ghosts.'

'Except in dreams.'

'Bad ones.'

At the mansion, he climbed the garden wall and found a perfect place for climbing to the basement roof. It wasn't too high off the ground and the cornerstones stuck out like ladders, giving him handholds and footholds. He dragged himself over the top, crawled along the flat surface to one of the dome-shaped skylights, sat next to it and brought down his boot heel, smashing the glass. It tinkled in the darkness below.

Forgetting the torch was a blunder. He couldn't see the floor and couldn't judge the height. He guessed not much higher than the climb he'd just made. He knocked away loose shards of glass and lowered himself through the opening, his arms at full stretch. Even in the fraction of a second it took to drop he realised it was much higher than he'd guessed. He thudded on the floor, the shock winding him. When his breathing returned to as near normal as it would ever be that night, he rose and walked slowly, feeling his way along the corridor walls.

The next panic came when he found the iron gate. It was padlocked.

'Fuck!'

'Don't go in if you don't know your way out, stupid.'

Anger moved him to try to kick it open, but he stopped himself, knowing he did not have the strength. He was about to turn back and look for an escape when he felt a draft of cool air coming from the unseen turnpike staircase to his left.

Pitch black inside, he tripped on the first step, but after his foot found the next one, the rest were easy all the way to the first floor.

The faint chinks of moonlight that shone through the edges of the shutters guided him through the rooms and he had no problem finding the painting. Even in that dull light the Lady sparkled, seeming to stand out from the canvas. He went to her, tilted the frame and fumbled around for wires and alarms. There were none.

A noise made him tense up again. He listened, but his breathing was the only sound.

Sure that his nerves were causing him to imagine all sorts of things he kept going, freeing the painting from its hook on the wall and carrying it to the window. He'd forgotten how heavy it was. Swapping the canvas for the fake would've been the smart move by far.

A welcome pane of moonlight spilled into the room as he unhinged the metal bar and opened the top shutters. And yet another relief when the window panel created no fuss, sliding down without much effort. He eased the painting out and lowered it to the sill and climbed out after it and continued down to the lower ledge, then reached up and gripped it and let it slide, scraping down the wall. The frame could be damaged, but that was no big deal.

The noise that he'd heard was a police car that had pulled up and cut its engine. He didn't know that until he turned a corner and almost bumped into one of the patrolling policemen.

'You were quick,' the policeman said. He levelled his torch then stumbled backwards, realising he wasn't talking to his buddy.

'What's that you've got?'

'A painting.'

'A painting?'

'Aye, a painting, see?'

As the policeman took hold of it, Alex let go and bolted.

His sense of bearings lost, he almost ran straight into the garden wall. He took three panicky attempts to get over it and then set off in the wrong direction towards the stable block. He doubled back through the bushes to the single-track road, turned down the gravel path and was soon over the bridge onto the mist-streaked golf course. He didn't have far to go, but the moonlight was making the mist glow all around him like a searchlight on the open ground.

With two fairways still to cross he heard a motor on the road he'd been on minutes earlier. He squatted and waited for it to pass. It didn't. It turned right onto the gravel path, two bobbing cones of light heading his way.

He had run no more than a few dozen strides when he heard it rasping over the bridge timbers, its engine changing to a squeal as it flew over the fairway mounds. It would be on him in seconds. Knowing it would do no good if they'd seen him, he dived into a greenside bunker, pressed himself under the lip and prayed that they hadn't.

The motor passed, then stopped. Not far.

Doors slid open, walkie-talkies crackled, and dogs barked.

His chest heaved. His breath steamed in the air. He tried not to breathe. He breathed into his sleeve. He breathed into the wet sand, said more prayers, and promised to pray more if he made it home. For no reason he imagined his first-year teacher, Binnie, saying he was always going to be a useless loser.

After the longest wait of his life, the minutes passing like days, the engine revved up and moved on. Carefully, he peered over the lip of the bunker and saw the taillights of a riot squad van as it crawled alongside the woods. It kept going and disappeared beyond the hill until the only sound was the hum of the diesel engines coming from the railway sheds. He lay on his side, dampness seeping through his clothes, as he waited for the moon to cloud over. When it did, he got to his feet and limped towards the woods, grimacing. His ankle had stiffened. He managed barely enough speed to pull himself up and over the mesh fence, rattling it.

Dogs barked.

'Got the bastard!'

'There!'

'In the bushes.'

'Suspect heading towards Corkerhill.'

That last shout echoed, squawking over at least four nearby walkie-talkies.

The fence rattled again and again. They were over it. Lots of them were over it.

He scrambled as fast as the pain in his ankle allowed, sensing every dip and turn of the path, using his arms to protect himself from the branches whipping at his face. He heard the cursing shouts of the policemen a good distance back and hoped to God that the brambles had them trapped. He took a moment to take the weight of his deadened ankle, leaning on a tree to steady himself, then mustered what was left of his second wind and scampered from the woods, across the field, into the housing scheme. He rubbed his eyes to shift the halos of yellow and orange that glowed around the streetlamps, found the gap in the hedging and crawled into the howf.

In the car seat, he huddled his knees, his cheek resting on the cold leather.

'Going for the painting was mental.'

'I don't trust myself with these daft ideas.'

'Hang on until they give up looking, then home to bed.'

He allowed his eyes to close.

The sound of no diesel engines spooked him awake, the crushing silence of it. The nightshift was over. He crawled out, leaving his hat and gloves in the howf. A few bedroom lights shone in the back gardens, dimmed red and orange by curtains. Not enough light to see clearly. He kept his head low to avoid the washing lines.

Out of nowhere came frenzied barking.

Then a man's shout.

'Police! Stay where you are!'

The stairs were only yards away.

'I'll set him on you!'

Alex chose to run.

He screamed as the dog clamped its jaw on his arm and brought him down.

In his shocked confusion his arm felt heavy and numb as if the dog was still holding on to him, yet he could see it, a snarling streak of fur and teeth and slobbers, tumbling in and out of the columns of light. His mind took time to engage. He was watching a dog fight.

More lights came on, neighbours were at their windows, dogs inside the houses going wild, and a policeman was clubbing Homeless, battering him. The big mongrel had hold of the squealing Alsatian by the neck and wouldn't let go.

Alex rose and shoulder barged, the weakest shoulder barge ever. It hardly budged the policeman who turned on his heels and swung the club, the blow glancing the inside of Alex's raised arm and striking his forehead.

Briefly unconscious, he came round with the clear impression that the next few moments had happened before — the smell of muddy grass, Missus Little helping him to his feet, Da snatching the club from the policemen and chucking it away, the policeman yelling into his radio for back up.

'Get upstairs son!' Da shouted.

The Alsatian was on its side, its tongue hanging to the ground. It raised its head and gave a weak growl as Alex hobbled past.

Admit Nothing

A distorted image of his face appeared in the chrome of the tap as he leaned to gulp from it, the white of his skull showing in the open cut above his eye.

At his back, Da came charging in. 'Let me see.'

He poured hot water and vinegar in a bowl and dabbed the wound. 'Tell me what happened, hurry.'

Alex couldn't think quickly enough.

'C'mon son. Tell me. They'll be at the door in a minute.'

'That painting. The one I told you about, the one in the mansion. I went to nick it and got chased. I hid, then ran back here.'

Da froze for a few seconds. Disbelief all over his face. 'Are you telling me you've been to Pollok House?'

Alex nodded.

'This morning?'

'Aye.'

'Jesus Christ! Have you lost your head?'

Heavy raps shook the front door.

'Right. Admit nothing. You were going out on the milk. That's what you say. Nothing else. Keep saying it, even if you need to say it a thousand times. You were on your way to your milk round. You hear?'

People watched from their windows as two police officers pressed Alex into the squad van, handcuffed. It seemed the whole building was up, except Ma. She hadn't seen any of this.

They took him to the accident and emergency at the Southern General and stood nearby while the doctor patched him up. Five stitches to the cut on his forehead, a bandage on his ankle, and two jabs, one on the backside. A wave of nausea rose in his stomach and he spewed the water that he had gulped earlier.

Da was at Brockburn Road police station when they brought him in. 'Look at the state of my son! An innocent boy, minding his own business and gets mauled and clubbed. You lot should be ashamed of—'

The sergeant banged the desk and shouted louder. 'On a night when three of my officers are injured on duty, you're lucky you're not being charged with police assault. Now shut it! He'll be in custody until we're good and done with him. Any more outbursts and you'll be banged up with him. Last warning.'

They took Alex's fingerprints and locked him in a disinfectant-smelling, graffiti-scraped cell.

Curled up on the concrete bed and failing to fight sleep, a horrible shivering dream came to him — a gang were dragging him to the road bridge, ready to drop him to the swollen river below. His mother was walking by, not seeing. He tried to call out to her but could not force a sound from his mouth. Then it came all at once, an echoing bawl that frightened him awake.

Keys rattled in the cell door, a policeman stepped inside, asked if he was okay, then led him to an interview room. A short while later Da showed up with a lawyer. Da sat next to Alex.

The lawyer stood. He spoke in a back-of-the-throat voice like the lawyers in court. 'The police have been patrolling Pollok Mansion House after a previous attempt, so they don't think this latest attempt was a haphazard one. Rather, it was well planned. They disturbed the intruder and chased him in the direction of Corkerhill. I brought about a good degree of embarrassment by reminding them they've had half the force out hunting for a professional art thief — the CID, the riot squad, dogs, and they find it fit to arrest the milk boy. It doesn't make a good report, particularly when you think of the extent of crime in this city. I expect they might want to keep it quiet.'

'What now?' Da asked.

'He's free to go. They'll check his prints and verify his milk round job in due course. It's normal procedure. They won't press charges provided you don't pursue any form of complaint, Mister Hannah.'

'Press charges for what? They've got no reason. They owe him an apology.'

'They'll think of a reason if it suits them, I can assure you.'

Coming out of the police station into the fresh April sunshine Alex experienced an overpowering sense of relief and a sudden burst of energy. Being off the hook was all that mattered.

Da soon put an end to that feeling. He let his hand rest on Alex's shoulder. 'We think of Peter every minute of every day, you know. We blame ourselves. Parents do that. They blame themselves for anything bad that happens to their kids. I fell to pieces, getting drunk, shutting myself off. I woke in the backcourts of the Gorbals one morning, my face burst from a fall, my clothes ripped and covered in muck and sick, kids laughing at me trying to find the energy to stand. All that mess when I should've been at home taking care of your mother. I owed it to her, to all of you, to get myself together. And now you're going off the rails. What on earth were you thinking? Look at me, Alex!'

'I don't know, honest. I thought I could help Ma get over Peter.'

'Come off it, son. You need your head straightened out. Your mother's learning to cope, but she'll never get over Peter. She doesn't have to, and that's the point. None of us do. We don't ever have to get over him because we'll always miss him. It'll always hurt, but we need to deal with it.'

Shame gripped Alex and his eyes welled.

'You're not looking at me! Who in a million years would've thought that you, a good boy from a good family, that you'd leave the house in the middle of the night to go and rob some place like you've no sense? Now, your mother knows nothing about this episode. I told her the same story that we told the polis. Stick to it. End the nonsense. You hear?'

'I hear, Da, I'm really sorry.'

'Don't be sorry, just start thinking straight.'

Ma answered the door. 'Good God! What have they done to you?' she said, wrapping her arms around him.

'He's had a bit of a fright. It's all sorted now. Mistaken identity.'

'A bloody liberty, that's what it is! I knew something like this would happen... out on the streets at that time in the morning. Didn't I say that? He's not going back on that milk run, and that's final. Tell him.'

'We're agreed. He's packing it in.'

Exhausted, Alex went to lie down but could not sleep for thinking there must be something seriously wrong with him — what normal boy would become obsessed with a painting, and what normal boy would be jealous of his brother for dying? He got up and went through to the kitchen.

When Ma set eyes on him she took his hands. 'I need you to promise me you'll take better care of yourself.'

'I promise.'

'We've had neighbours at the door,' Da said. 'They saw you being hit. Saw it with their own eyes and they're ready to swear witness.'

Alex pulled on his boots.

'Where are you going?' Ma said, worry all over her face.

'To Homeless.'

'Don't be long. It's better if you stay inside with me for a while.'

'I will, Ma.'

He soaked two slices of bread in the frying pan fat and took them downstairs but could not find the dog. He knocked on doors. It was Missus Little who mentioned the Cat and Dog Home. They usually give them a few days before having them destroyed, she said. She found the number in the phone book, dialled it and passed the receiver to Alex. He described Homeless as a big mongrel that had been in a fight, yellow fur with mangy bits. The operator, a girl, relayed the description to someone in the background.

A man came on the line. 'Sounds like the big beast I picked up this morning. Someone called it in. Nae collar. Lying in a field with head wounds. I thought he'd been hit by a truck. Thought he'd gone there to die.'

'He's mine.'

'Come and get him. Save us the trouble of putting him to sleep. You'll need to see to him though, keep dressing his wounds and that.'

'I'll see to him, mister, don't worry.'

Through Walls

Da's proudly weather-beaten skin, brown as a nut and wrinkled, came from working outdoors and gave him the appearance of someone who knew his stuff when talking about gardening. He had placed an ad in the newsagent window and talked himself into a few jobs in Mosspark. His name soon got around, and he took on more jobs, including some in Newlands and Giffnock with gardens the size of football pitches, enough to keep busy throughout the summer months. Alex and Forbes helped during the school break. The three of them walked to work, arrived around half nine, stopped at half twelve for cheese rolls and tea from a flask, then toiled on until four. Da gave the orders, explaining the different plants, spacing for shrubs, how to double dig, how to sharpen mowers and shears. Alex had a feeling that getting them involved was a plan to keep them out of trouble.

The only crime the two brothers committed that summer was sneaking on the golf course in the evenings, when the last of the golfers were making their way to the clubhouse. Two clubs and a putter between them, they played pitch and putt until the light faded around eleven o'clock on cloudless summer nights.

The antiques still came to mind from time to time. Alex's frustration over them was fading, but it was hard to block them out completely. He only wanted to know. Nothing else.

His new drive was to get into university. Miss Cleghorn had helped him catch up with the lessons. She gave him copies of past exam papers, explained what he needed to learn, and he set about learning it, studying hard, especially early the mornings when he had the house to himself. The results came through the post in late July. He had passed all the exams with room to spare.

After school started back in August, she invited him to a 'study evening' at her place, along with a bunch of fifth-year boys and girls. He wanted to look his best. He shone his shoes and took a long soak in the bath and shaved his first shave, cutting his chin, twice, with his father's razor. The splash of aftershave nipped like mad and reddened his face.

Ma called through from the kitchen as he was looking for his best shirt. 'It's in here. In the ironing bundle,' she said, like she could see through walls. She stood holding it at the tip of her finger, giving him a look that he hadn't seen for years, her funny-curious face, one eyebrow raised and one lowered. He left in an excellent mood because of that.

Miss Cleghorn's place was a high-ceiling hippy flat in Bath Street smelling of incense and furnished with a jungle of houseplants and rugs and cushions. The group, six pupils and

Miss Cleghorn, who wanted to be called by her first name, Deborah, sat round an oak table in the kitchen talking about books and foreign countries and music. She had a way of firing them up, and they had an opinion on everything. Alex offered a comment on George Best's return to training after quitting. It did not bring much response apart from Miss Cleghorn getting on her favourite subject, entertaining them with stories of people who had wasted their amazing talents.

Even the meal she made was special. Spaghetti, warm bread and a glass of red wine was far from anything he'd had at home. The wine, she said, was French, a wee taste for cultural reasons. Not sure of how to tackle spaghetti, he thought he looked a clown having to suck strands into his mouth and splashing tomato sauce over his shirt.

She stood at the sink and offered him a wet cloth. 'Try using a fork and spoon,' she whispered. 'Follow my lead.'

Nathan had decided to give art school another go and was due to head off to London at the end of September. His going-away party was jammed with his aunts, uncles, cousins and a few of his arty pals, standing around in groups chatting and drinking. The only person missing was Nathan.

Shona and Rita were playing the music.

'Hey,' Alex said to them, trying to be cool. 'How's it going?'

'Hay's for horses,' Shona replied.

'Okay, horse. How's it going? Ha ha.'

'Very funny.'

'You taking requests?' he asked.

'Got one in mind?' Rita said.

'Aye, nae more Bay City Rollers.'

'D'you know who you're like?' Shona said. 'See those swots on *University Challenge*? That's you.'

'Is that right? Well, d'you know those women that hang around—'

Rita nudged him. 'Oh, you better not say that, Alex Hannah.' She held up her empty glass. 'Get me a refill, please. A cider.'

'Me too,' Shona said.

As he was pouring the drinks in the kitchen Missus Coghlin put her arm round his waist. She was half-cut. She pulled him in close. 'Do me a favour, love. Go to the lock-up and bring back muggins. He's done a bunk.'

After serving the ciders, Alex set off. He went at a jog, wanting to get back quickly and hoping for a second chance with Shona.

He found Nathan packing painting tools into a battered old briefcase.

'Alright Alex.'

'Your mammy sent me. Says you've to come back and entertain your guests. Says it's an embarrassment, doing a runner from your own party.'

'I needed to get away for a wee puff. It's pretty crap, sure it is?'

'It's alright, but I don't know too many people.'

'You know Shona and what's-her-name?'

'Rita.'

'Aye, Rita,' Nathan said. He offered Alex the last of his joint. 'Want a puff?'

'Nah, it'll do my head in.'

'I'm told they're letting bold boy loose.'

'Aye. I hear he's getting married. He's a daddy now.'

'You best man?'

'I'm looking forward to catching up and that... I've got something to sort out with him, but best man? Nae chance. It's the short straw. You've got to buy a suit for a start and make a speech. I'll tell him to ask you instead.'

'I'll be long gone. The Royal College of Art. How does that sound? My own digs and loads of gorgeous talent in London.'

'I'm jealous.'

'I need to find a part-time job in a bar or something to help pay for my keep. My old man says it'll make me or break me, like I'm joining the army, the old halfwit... By the way, I don't suppose you want a keepsake?'

'What's that?'

'A wee memento of your run-in with the law.'

'The fake? Don't think so. I've had enough of that. You could always give it to Jamie as a wedding present.'

Nathan let out a coughing laugh. 'I couldnae believe you actually went and tried to nick it. I never really thought you had the nerve. You should've waited till I finished the copy and swapped it during the day like I told you.'

'Where is it anyhow?'

'In my attic. I hope Jamie wants it. I don't want all that effort to have been for nothing.'

'I know. I still get nightmares about that night.'

'I'm not talking about your mad effort. I'm talking about my artistic endeavour. I put my soul into that painting I'll have you know. It'd be a shame seeing it going to waste. It's better than the original.'

'Nae point in being shy eh?'

'I'm doing okay. Sold my Bob Dylan portrait to a guy who owns a nightclub. Twenty quid and two tickets to see the Stones. Cannae wait.'

'They're meant to be amazing. Who's getting the other one?'

'You, if you want?'

'Too right. How much?'

'Don't be daft. It's yours.'

Diced Glass

Alex's first rock concert should have been a lasting memory of the jumping crowd, the lights, the music that thumped in your chest, the energy of it all. It wasn't. He remembered that night for another reason. After leaving the Apollo, he and Nathan were strolling down Renfield Street in the same direction as the city traffic heading for the Southside. They were buzzing over the concert, talking about buying the new album when they noticed a man walking between the lines of cars. He was coming through the exhaust fumes that hung low in the damp air, pushing his palms towards the ground — signalling to the drivers to slow down. Further along, a crowd was gathering on the road outside the Central Station. A car had run into the back of a van. It took a few moments for Alex to realise that, at the centre of it all were two people, one of them in a heap, the other, a girl, kneeling. As he got closer, he recognised Lorna.

In the weeks and months that followed, he met her several times and her story never changed. Jamie had kept himself to himself in borstal, obeyed the rules, kept in with the guards, kept up with the brutal drills and worked hard at the building-trade lessons. After his release he took an interview for an apprentice cabinetmaker, got offered the job and was ready to start the following Monday — four days in the factory and one at Anniesland College on a City and Guilds course. It was Jamie who suggested that it would be good for them to go out and celebrate, have some time to themselves. Lorna's mother would take care of the baby for a while.

Lorna's unease at leaving the baby grew once they were in town. She didn't want to spend two hours in a cinema and wasn't interested in the discos, so they settled for a café and sat talking over their wedding plans before heading off to catch a train. Arm in arm on the steps of Central Station, they stepped aside as a mob of boys came charging down through the crowd. One of them, a boy of twelve or thirteen, bumped Lorna, dipped her handbag and made off with her purse. Jamie chased and caught him on the road, forced him against the parked van and was frisking him for the purse when the gang attacked.

They dragged Jamie to the ground, kicking and punching.

Screaming at them, Lorna forced her way through and stood with her feet at either side of his head protecting him. It lasted only a few seconds, and they were gone.

Jamie rose to his feet, winded. A kidney punch, he said, holding his back, but when he brought his hand out from inside his jacket blood dripped from his fingertips. Lorna's legs buckled at the sight of it at his feet. It was running down the inside of his trousers, over his shoes and onto the ground. He stumbled backward. A car swerved to miss him and smashed into the van.

Alex saw what happened next. Blood was spreading out from under Jamie, seeping through the pieces of diced windscreen glass that sparkled in the streetlights. Lorna's hands were on his cheeks. She was pleading, mouthing something that Alex couldn't hear. The adults in the crowd were shaking their heads at each other, sharing a lack of hope for the body on the road.

A black taxi didn't slow. It overtook the line of cars, splashing blood on Alex and Nathan and the onlookers. Men cursed and shouted and shook their fists at it.

The story in the newspapers said that a 16-year-old father, James Bryce, was stabbed to death in a gang fight in the city centre, and that another 16-year-old, Jake Armstrong, had been charged with murder.

Every Drop of Light

On a Saturday evening in the middle of February 2013, Alex was flicking through a magazine while waiting for *Match of the Day* to start on telly. His wife had gone to bed an hour earlier with her book, and their youngest daughter was out on the town. He would not sleep until she was home. Vaguely aware that the television panellists were discussing the next-day's newspapers, he heard someone say, 'Qianlong period vase.'

He reached for the remote.

'A new world record, apparently.'

'The family who found it in a cardboard box in the attic are still pinching themselves.'

'The seller knew there was keen interest in this prized piece of Chinese porcelain even before it appeared at auction, although No one could have predicted anything near the cool twenty million it fetched at auction.'

'What do you think of that reaction by the Chinese bidders?'

'It's further proof of their booming economy, allowing their trophy-hunters to win the auction-house battles and bring home their cultural rarities. It's all about their national identity and pride.'

'They're also buying a few of our good footballers, another rarity these days judging by the England team's performance,' said a less-interested panellist.

'It's time to clear out those attics and sheds. You never know what might turn up,' the presenter concluded, before reading out a headline on the Euro crisis.

Alex booted-up his laptop and typed in *Priceless Chinese Vase.* Six of them appeared on the screen. The first piece of blurb told a story he already knew, all about a Glasgow couple using a precious Ming vase as a lamp stand until they saw an identical one in the Burrell Museum. It sold for hundreds of thousands in the early 1980s, a time when he was beginning his career as a property lawyer and had persuaded himself that it was only a coincidence, resisting the temptation to go snooping around.

Clicking on hyperlinks, he came across umpteen stories of ancient artefacts selling for silly money. He glanced at his watch, stopped what he was doing to send his daughter a text offering her a lift, which he knew she wouldn't accept, and then got back to his search.

An hour later a taxi pulled up, and his daughter and two of her friends came through the house giggling, said hello and disappeared into the kitchen. He continued to scour the websites. He remembered all the stolen-stolen items: the vases, the gold

Madonna, the gemstone cups, the owl-shaped flask, the Buddha, the dragon-headed candlestick holder, the dog with the pig's tail, the winged horse and rider and the jade-stone bear.

So far, the Burrell Museum's website gave the only firm connection — a photograph of a lion's head sculpture in black stone, bigger, otherwise identical to the one he remembered, described as the head of an Egyptian goddess who protected the pharaohs. He looked at his watch again, 4:15. He powered-off and went to bed.

In the morning, while his wife was at church, he put his dog, an Alsatian called Talen, into the back of his battered old jeep and drove towards Glasgow. Sundays were usually kept for visiting his mother at Sarah's house in Stirling. He called her instead and arranged to visit during the week.

The excitement that had kept him up for half the night helped the two-hour drive pass quickly. It was a trip he had to get out of his system. He parked outside the railway depot in Corkerhill and walked round the street, keeping the dog on the leash. The howf was well and truly gone along with the tenements, replaced by neat privately owned houses. He thought of the kids he'd grown up with, and how alike they were at that time, adapting to their own situations in their own ways. Jamie's death struck him then, harder than it did at any time in the past, a wave of emotion that gripped and choked. 'Christ!' he said out loud. 'Where did that come from?'

McPeat came to mind. No-one had seen him since Borstal. Rumours had him on the other side of the world owning one of the largest fleets of ice cream vans in Australia. If that were true, how did he come by the start-up cash? On second thoughts, if that were true, then good on him.

He headed over the motorway footbridge onto a tarmac path that passed the farmhouse and led along the river. Unshaven, wearing khaki shorts, walking boots and a heavy winter jacket he did not look out of place amongst the dog-walkers in Pollok Country Park, as they now called it.

Cutting across Haggs Castle Golf Course he could see how the new road, the M77, had transformed the landscape. He hoped the priceless artefacts weren't buried underneath. Hard to believe that the city councillors had allowed a motorway to be carved through the park, destroying so much of the forest. He remembered the legal arguments — the Stirling-Maxwells had gifted the land to the care of Glasgow Corporation on condition that it remain forever as open parkland for the benefit of the citizens, or words to that effect. Still, Alex knew too well that barristers could find a loophole in almost any legal document relating to gifted or bequeathed land, even designated greenbelt considered as the best park in Europe, and they would do it for a small fortune. Money and power seldom lost a court case. It took half of Strathclyde police force to shift the encamped eco-warrior protestors from the treetops in a dawn raid. Emergency response teams and officers on climbing ropes with chain cutters, all for a motorway that added to the most frequently announced traffic jam on UK radio, the Kingston Bridge.

And before the motorway, more than ten years before construction started, the golf course committee took bullying action by extending the fairways and blocking-off the historic path to the park, preventing access from Corkerhill, and breaching umpteen laws and regulations, in his opinion.

While getting himself worked up over those injustices, the idyllic railway village came to mind. Its demolition must have been up there with Glasgow Corporation's most wasteful development ideas.

All this complaining. It must be an age thing.

The paths in the forest next to the motorway were gone, swamped with brambles. No-one walked there any longer, and it was difficult to find your bearings.

He stumbled on a pile of rubble behind the remaining length of the mesh fence at the edge of the forest. A likely place for hiding the duffel bags if you walked in a straight line from the railway turntable. He moved rocks around, tumbling them over. Even though he had searched many years before, he had a powerful feeling that at least some of the antiques were still buried in the park. There were no signs, not near the surface anyway. He'd buy a metal detector, that's what he'd do, the best on the market, a Pin-seeker, the Rolls Royce of metal detectors. And he'd ask Forbes for an opinion, although he could guess Forbes's reply, 'Behave yourself.'

He found his way to the fallen sycamore. The only trace of it was the root crater, barely visible under the withered fern leaves. He took a detour to the Burrell Museum, built on the pavilion picnic area. It looked like a giant conservatory, apart from the medieval entrance that had been taken from some old castle. He walked back along the tree-lined roadway between the fields of Highland cows. Once at the mansion, he leashed the dog to the railings, stroked him and spoke to him, saying he'd only be gone for ten minutes. He grudgingly paid the National Trust's entry fee and went inside.

The place was heaving with tourists, most of them queuing for tables in the basement restaurant.

Upstairs, on the first floor, National Trust guides hung around in every room, smartly dressed men and women who talked as if they were experts on the history of the mansion. He spent a few minutes chatting to them as he made his way to the library and the painting.

A guide, an elderly woman with a white powdery face, rose from her chair and stood at his side.

'It's an El Greco,' she said.

He nodded.

'Both mantel paintings are by El Greco, although this one causing all the fuss.'

'Oh. In what way?'

'It's unsigned, and experts say that the tone and brush strokes are inconsistent with El Greco's usual style. You can see that by comparing it with the *Portrait of a Man* on the other mantel. He's dull and boring and looks as old as the painting itself, whereas she's young and vigorous and colourful. They've debated her and studied her, even X-rayed her.'

'Did it prove anything?'

'The curator called us to a meeting and told us there can be no doubting the painting's authenticity, that it's a timeless masterpiece, the most valuable and most loved item in the collection. Although, I doubt we will ever put an end to the rumours and speculation.'

Alex looked closer at the *Lady in a Fur Wrap*. Even after all these years, he was certain she had gained an extra touch of colour.

'That couldn't be lipstick she's wearing, could it?'

'I wouldn't have thought so,' the guide replied, and returned to her seat.

Alex left, planning to contact his old friend. From what he'd read in the newspaper, Nathan was exhibiting his latest works at a gallery in Knightsbridge, London.

*

Dedicated to James Paterson, a friend and Hardridge boy who died young.

Acknowledgements

To Lucy Anne, Matthew and Thomas, for their common sense input.

To Bill and Annette Gurney, Mary Paul and Gerry Mclean for taking time to critique the manuscript and for their advice.

A special thanks to Bill Gurney, who gave the morale-boosting review shown on the back cover. Bill, an Etonian, and retired Head of English at King Edward VI Aston School, Birmingham, had an upbringing entirely different to that of the characters in this story. 'I wonder which of us had the most interesting childhood,' he remarked.

Jamie's Keepsake

Jamie's Keepsake

Printed in Great Britain
by Amazon